Planet Thirteen

Adiu & Jotre

D1714061

Planet Thirteen

Adiu & Jotre

Jacobie Wirick

Planet Thirteen ~ Wenona & Ateg will be published later this year.

For Alton:

My contracted partner,

greatest supporter,

best human friend, and more.

Planet Thirteen

Adiu & Jotre

Part One: Adiu & Jotre

Chapter 1

"I need a contracted union partner," Adiu tells her brother in City Speak after the Evening Meal, sitting at the table in the dining area.

"When will you tell Mama and Papa about needing a partner?" Ateq asks, also in City Speak.

Adiu and Ateq talk in City Speak at home for private conversations. Their parents insisted their academic studies were taught in City Speak, the language of those who lived in the domed cities and towns. A private teacher came to their homestead during their Primary School years. Their ancestral tongue is written and spoken within their orthodox community and at

Mama's and Papa's homestead.

Equo, their mama, is placing slices of Adiu's fiftieth birthday cake on small plates at the kitchen island. Their papa, Iuot, is getting the small crystal glasses from the china cabinet in the far corner of the sitting room.

Adiu replies, "I will tell them tonight after the birthday celebration."

"Asking if you prayed about needing a partner will be Mama's first question," Ateq says.

Adiu says, "I have prayed for twenty-eight days during all three of my Wisdom studies, as Fir On requires."

"I am happy for you and for me. Once you are contracted, I will also be available to partner with someone," says Ateq.

Their parents return with cake and glasses of fermented fruit juice. Adiu and Ateq stand up as each is handed a crystal glass.

In their ancestral tongue, in unison, they all say, "Fir On, we thank you for your constant watch over us. You bless us with your great bounty. For this, we are and will always be grateful."

They raise their glasses and lower them to their mouths, taking in their contents. This potent drink is called "hooch". It is used for medicinal and ceremonial events only.

Ateq, Mama, and Papa sit down. Adiu remains standing.

Adiu says, "After twenty-eight days, Fir On answered my prayers. I am asking for my birthright as your firstborn child."

Adiu takes her seat, waiting for Mama's reaction. Their parents look at each other. To Adiu, their silence is almost deafening.

Mama stands up and walks away from the table. Papa bows his head. Adiu looks toward her brother. Ateq raises his shoulders, indicating he doesn't know what is happening either. They sit and wait.

Eventually, Mama returns from their bed chamber. There are tears in her eyes. She stands behind Adiu, removing the hair from around her left ear. A curved clip in the shape of a butterfly slides into place at the top of her ear. Adiu remains perfectly still, not knowing what is happening. Mama's lips move in a silent prayer. A firm pinch radiates from the very top edge of her left ear. It is followed by another one lower down and to the left. Adiu can feel strands of metal touching the back of her ear. She reaches up to touch the clip and the strands. Mama hands her a small mirror from her dress pocket.

Adiu looks at the clip for the first time. A golden butterfly sits gently on the outer edge of her ear. Its body is resting against its curve. There are two emerald studs in holes at the head and tail where Mama pierced her ear. These are held in place by small backs built within the butterfly's body behind Adiu's ear. The strands are connected there in a line. There are thirteen of them. They are different lengths and end in a straight line a few inches below her ear.

Taking the farthest one in her hand, Adiu reads the round

disc at its end. The first line reads, "Equo Udon Uoea." The second line reads, "Iuot Otau Udos." The third line reads, "2106". Adiu begins to cry softly. Papa wipes tears from his eyes on his sleeve. Ateq clears his throat loudly, looking away for a moment.

Returning to her place at the table, Mama says, "Today, you have taken your place as the Firstborn of the fourteenth generation of Aviqa and Aviqi, the thirteenth couple created by the Fir On. The butterfly represents your growth from a child into a woman. You follow in their footsteps." Unable to control her emotions, Mama sits down and leans her face into Papa's shoulder.

Ateq leaves the table and returns with a jug of fermented fruit juice. "This requires a toast," he says, refilling the small glasses. Everyone stands.

Ateq says, "To my sister, the Firstborn."

The glasses are raised, and the liquid shoots back. Adiu remains standing as the other three return to their seats.

Mama and Papa have been waiting for this moment since Adiu was born. They chose to sell their pair of thoroughbred horses shortly after her arrival. Even a champion boar and its sow were sold at the quarterly auction. Instead of hosting an elaborate celebration feast, typical for the arrival of the Firstborn, the extended family came together to provide simple, homemade dishes for a shared buffet. From then on, Adiu and her parents continue to sell one-half of the homestead's annual yield to provide for her future. As the Firstborn, Adiu is entitled to one-half of all of the homestead's inventory, including equipment, livestock, seeds, and other materials. Waiting for twenty-six years after graduating from Secondary School gave the family time to weather the leaner years and benefit from the more bountiful ones. Being a direct female descendant of Aviqa and Aviqi, whose firstborn children maintain the ways of *The No Fir* and are blessed for their endeavors through twelve generations, afforded Adiu's maternal grandmother the ability to pay her Secondary School expenses without incurring debt.

"This blessing comes with a caveat: I need to find a contracted union partner," Adiu says. Mama and Papa exchange shocked looks.

Ateq breaks the silence, "It is about time; I thought my turn may never come. Don't you think so?" The question hangs in the air.

"Are you sure Fir On made this requirement? Because you have lived alone for so long after Secondary School, Mama and I thought Fir On wanted it to be so. We knew you would want to move out one day, and we have made plans to assist you with your homestead," Papa says.

Adiu sits down, taking a moment to gather her thoughts. "Mama and Papa, I appreciate that you planned for me to live alone. While I was at Secondary School, I fell ill with a disease brought on by a young town dweller child whose family visited.

The city and town dwellers get several illnesses during childhood, but they receive shots to lessen the effects. Homesteaders do not have a way to fight these illnesses. The disease infected all the homestead faculty and students who had remained during the winter break. It left all of us unable to have children. I am barren."

Mama comes over and hugs her daughter tightly. Adiu rubs Mama's arms and falls into her embrace.

Adiu continues, "After much prayer, I saw this as an opportunity to devote myself to Fir On. I have lived a celibate life and have received many blessings. I came back to our homestead and practiced the skills I learned. When praying about my birthright, Fir On's blessing came with this requirement: I need to find a partner to share the responsibility."

Mama says, "Fir On has spoken. We will meet later to discuss the details of your inheritance. Right now, let's raise a toast to your future partner."

Papa fills the glasses for a third time. The discussion that follows concerns the contracted partnership process.

***

The following day, Adiu begins the first step in finding a suitable contracted union partner. She requests matchmaking services through a telegram to the Matron Family Services. While others provided these services, her family has utilized the women of this Matron family for as long as they have practiced their craft. These women are known widely for their thorough research and ability to maneuver through the rugged terrain of human interactions.

Adiu receives a telegram in return:

Lancaster Telegram & Telephone Co.

To: Adiu Equo Iuot
From: Matron Family Services

Adiu,

I have received your Contracted Partnership Service form. I am willing to consider your request. Please complete the questionnaire included in The No Fir. Upon my review, I will contact you with my decision. Please include an inventory of the dowry you will bring to the partnership.

Sincerely, Matron Qyn

Adiu's lips move in constant prayer as she copies and completes the questionnaire's multiple forms and proofs of their information authenticity, sitting at the dining area table. Its pages include a family tree and supporting documentation, union partner requirements, and a dowry agreement. Due to Adiu's willingness to consider a town dweller, the City or Town dweller interaction form must also be completed. If, at this point, Matron Qyn takes on her request, Adiu will travel to her office to meet, sign a contract for her services, and make a down payment. Only then will Matron Qyn begin the search for her union partner. Adiu will make an additional payment as each step proceeds.

Chapter 2

Qyn, the Matron assigned to Adiu's request, understands the responsibility of her task. Adiu's dowry amounts to over 550,000 colonial units. Although Qyn has seen more significant amounts, they are from upper-class city dwellers. Two specific sections in the application give her pause: Adiu's requirements for a partner and her experience in the city. Qyn makes notes on her copy of these documents, places them into a folder, and files the folder in the work-in-progress bin on her office desk.

My Requirements

1. He must have grown up on an underground homestead and be willing to live as *The No Fir* requires, including monogamy until death.

Issues:

A. The first section of requirement Number One is the easiest. After thirteen generations of homesteaders living with or near city dwellers, homestead families decrease steadily. Two factors counterbalanced this: Homesteaders need as many hands as possible, and they enjoy the process of making their own.

B. The remainder of requirement one is more complicated. Finding a true practitioner of the orthodoxy will require tracking down a male who can trace his lineage back to the original thirteen couples or someone willing to take up this commitment with unwavering dedication. The assimilation of homesteaders into the services of the nearby cities and towns has led to many of them living underground in apartments near shuttle and train lines. Middle children are most likely to make up their number since they do not receive the advantages of being first or the responsibilities of being last. They have a sustainable income and the perks of living under the domes. With the right of choice between the risks associated with homesteading or the service industry without family reprisal, more firstborn children are joining their middle siblings. They are even making their way into the town communities and city societies. With such mingling comes a desire to fit in and abandon tradition, mainly when orthodox.

2. He has not been in a union previously.

Issues:

A. Some homesteaders are more liberal, forsaking this requirement.

B. Orthodox male widowers are not an option.

C. A partner near her age may have been in a union where their partner or they broke the contract.

3. He must also be a firstborn, but not an only child, and without family obligations upon the commencement of our union.

Issues:

A. Unlike their siblings, there is only one firstborn per family generation.

B. Not being an Only Child limits the possibilities even more.

4. He must be at least thirteen years younger than me.

Issues:

A. At her age, her possible partners can be, at the most, thirty-seven years old.

B. Due to requirement number five, the average age for graduating from Secondary School is twenty-six years.

C. Too young a potential candidate is less likely to be her definition of a partner and may want to have biological children. See requirement number seven.

5. He must be a secondary school graduate in a field of study practical for utilization on a homestead, with a grade point average of one hundred thirty out of the maximum one hundred sixty-nine possible points or higher. This degree should be in the agricultural and vocational fields.

Issues:

A. Most homesteaders are forgoing a Secondary education; instead, they are apprenticing under their parents or family.

B. Most homestead families need their children's labor or are monetarily unable to fund Secondary School expenses adequately.

6. He must understand that he and I will work in partnership, but I will be the head of the household and responsible for final decision-making.

Issues:

A. Adiu must understand that if she wants a true partner, she must be willing to make compromises and regularly consider another person's point of view.

B. She must also know that being the head of the household will not mean anything if her partner is not willing to accept her as such.

C. Partnerships are built on mutual respect and the ability to learn from your partner.

7. As I am barren, he should not expect to be a father, except for the adoption of children I agree upon.

Issues:

A. See requirement number four.

B. She may be giving false hope with the second section.

8. He must show evidence of his ability to create needed products from raw resources, knowledge of homesteading skills, and adaptability to unforeseen circumstances.

Issues:
A. What type of evidence?
B. How will he show this evidence?
C. What kind of products?
D. What level of expertise?
E. What homesteading skills is she requiring?
F. How diverse does this knowledge need to be?
G. Does she understand the limitations?
H. What does she mean by adaptability?
I. What does she mean by unforeseen circumstances?
J. What are acceptable adaptability levels?
K. Can she give specific examples of each?

9. He must be willing to care for my needs and wants until his death.
Issues: I could be dead before discussing and solving all the problems.

10. These are the minimal requirements for a contracted union and are non-negotiable.
Issues: See requirement nine.

11. Additional requirements can and will be added up to its finalization.
Issues: See all the above.

Interactions with Town and City Dwellers

My grandfather built a carved, ornate chest and presented it to me at eleven upon graduating from primary school. The chest held all my possessions when I traveled to Secondary School. Traveling by train, my journey would take over a month. My chest had been given a tag by the train conductor and loaded into a baggage car with the rest of the passengers' larger containers. Sneaking a peek inside another baggage car, high stacks of many unusual things filled its space: wooden fermented fruit and beer barrels, steel cargo boxes of all sizes, cages with bars and air holes that hold all types of farm animals, tall wardrobes, dining and kitchen tables, storage cabinets, and cardboard boxes marked with fragile signs containing appliances. I could not take everything in at once.

All of a sudden, someone grabs my hips. Whirling around, my eyes meet those of this filthy, wrinkled older man very close to mine. He holds my hips tightly and laughs. Lifting my hands from my sides, I place them on each of his shoulders and shove them as hard as possible. Staggering backward, he begins to fall. At the last moment, another worker catches him. The others laugh.

Their supervisor says, "Leave the passengers alone and get back to work. Charlie, I am docking you an hour's pay for that stunt."

Turning, I run toward the nearest train conductor. Seeing what happened, he says, "Elliot, please escort this young lady to the second-class carriage number six. Ask Darius to take extra care of her." A second train conductor holds out his elbow. I grab Elliot's elbow like my life depended upon him.

I hear the first train conductor say, "Ralph if you cannot keep your men under control, I will file a conduct report with the main office. See how long you stay as a supervisor then. Charlie, you have been warned about such behavior before. It will not be so funny when you cannot feed your wife and five kids. The rest of you get back to work now."

Elliot holds out his hand to help me up the stairs to the vestibule of the sleeping car. Picking up my skirt and grabbing the rail on the right side, I ascend the narrow steel stairs. Racing to the back, I stand with my back tight against the other train door. I can only watch as Elliot helps other passengers onto the train. I hear the train whistle blow. He picks up his little stool from the platform and climbs the stairs. A section of the vestibule floor falls into place. Elliot closes and locks the train door. Only when he lightly touches my elbow and points toward the sleeping car do I feel like I can move. My anger and fear become shame. With a bowed head, following Elliot, I enter the sleeping carriage.

When we arrive, the sleeping car porter, Darius, is waiting. He speaks the ancestral tongue. Another young lady will be my dining companion. She is traveling to a different Secondary School farther down the train line. She will join the train after the Midday Meal the next day.

A small leather-covered book provides information about the activities aboard the train, their scheduled times, the porter's duties, when he would perform them, and the amenities available. Darius's voice is soft and calming as he reads the book's details. He points out information specifically related to me. By the time Darius leaves, the effects of the incident are behind me.

Adiu Equo Inot

***

During their meetings, Adiu intently listens when Qyn speaks, carefully and honestly answers when questioned, and is willing to compromise when she finds pertinent information realistic and logical. Still, she stands her ground when passionate about her ideas and beliefs. After nearly eleven months, a possible partner's application arrives at the Matron's office. His name is Aeat Ueqi Atau. He fulfills almost all of Adiu's requirements. Now, Qyn and her staff begin the process in earnest.

Chapter 3

Adiu secures a modest apartment in the city as her first meeting with Aeat approaches. It contrasts with the spacious homestead where her grandparents, parents, and two children live. Although both are underground, the new apartment at the end of a shuttle line is a significant departure from the homestead.

Limited monthly utilities are included in her rent. Adiu keeps records of her monthly usage to stay within these limits. Living on her parents' homestead prepares her well. Her usage in the first three months allows her to adjust her habits, including weekly baths with salts and lotion. Her apartment also includes a dishwasher, clothing washer and dryer. She avails herself of the clothes washer but dries her clothing in a large closet attached to her sleeping chamber and spritzes homemade fabric scent on them. She purchases a carved dressing table and chair. Their curves and swirls nearly match the ones on her chest. She replaces the steel iron passed down through the women in her family with an electric model. The older model resides in the chest and will return to her homestead. She repeats this process with other electrical appliances. Decisions about which will be sold can wait. She always travels to her parents' homestead, knowing they will not approve these purchases. She balances these with homemade items she and her family created.

A dedicated section of the local library is devoted to educating homesteaders living in underground apartments like hers. Adiu diligently checks out these books and takes copious notes in her journal, feeling like she has returned to Secondary School. Her daily meetings with other homestead women and men at the library and tea rooms inspire Adiu to search for those with the highest level of dedication. If she is still looking for a suitable group, Adiu seeks advice from people in her library and travels to other libraries based on their recommendations. A journal entry reads:

"All people on Planetary Thirteen follow a schedule based on its orbit around its binary suns and rotation. It takes 364 rotational cycles to complete one orbit, an orbital year. The year is divided into four seasons. Each season is ninety-one rotational cycles long. These are called rotational days. The rotational days are divided into thirteen ninety-minute rotational hours. Each rotational hour is the time it takes the planet to rotate across each time zone. The planetary acceptance of chronological time provides for an interconnectedness negotiated in the Great Schism Treaty signed on Planetary Ten. Each rotational day starts at 2:45, with the morning meal lasting until 3:45. A morning work session occurs from 3:45 to 6:00. Between 6:00 and 7:00, the midday meal takes place. The afternoon work session begins at 7:00 and continues until 9:45. The evening meal lasts from 9:45 until 10:45. Rest time starts at 10:45 until 2:45 the next day."

***

Aeat's family calls him Jotre. Adiu will honor this family tradition. Qyn is the only one who has seen her traveling clothes, so she wears them to her first meeting with Jotre. Wearing his green traveling suit, Jotre waits in Qyn's meeting room. He and Qyn rise from their seats. Jotre bows toward Adiu. She bows toward Qyn and then him. Adiu stands beside her chair and waits. Qyn clears her throat a few seconds later. Jotre takes his cue, pulls out her chair, and seats Adiu. Two staff members enter the room. Each bows toward Qyn. One lifts the white porcelain teapot, looking directly at her. After a nod, the staff member refills Qyn's tea cup and adds two sugar cubes before setting his sight on Adiu. She also nods, and the second staff member goes to a sideboard, returning with a matching teacup, spoon, and saucer, and places a lace silk napkin in Adiu's lap. Finally, the second staff member refills Jotre's cup with the steaming hot liquid from a coffee pot. A plate of petit four appears at Adiu's left elbow.

Qyn introduces Adiu Equo Iuot, the fourteenth-generation firstborn daughter of Equo Udon Uoea, the thirteenth-generation second-born daughter, and her partner Iuot Otau Udos, third-born son... until arriving at the thirteenth of the first couple, Aviqa and Aviqi, created by Fir On. Next, the presentation of Aeat Ueqi Atau's (Jotre Jotu Mara's) lineage, and for the next two hours, written ancestry questions and answers are submitted to the Matron. A clock chimes somewhere outside the building. The three rise in unison; Aeat replaces the chairs of Qyn and Adiu under the table in order, opens the office door, and waits as the ladies leave the room.

During the Midday Meal, Adiu continues her daily Wisdom Studies and prayers. Aeat creates a list:

1. *The women in my former relationships held modern ideas.*
2. *Beyond possible marriage, there were few expectations.*
3. *Does she know that I am not a virgin?*
4. *How much will this matter to her?*
5. *Is she aware of those other relationships? If so, how much?*

Aeat is still compiling his list when a staff member lightly taps the door. He says, "Come in."

"Sir, the Matron has returned to the meeting room. Ms. Adiu Equo Iuot states she will be there shortly," the staff member says.

"Thank you," Aeat says, realizing his food is untouched. He tries to shake the doubts from his mind before leaving the room.

When Aeat enters, Qyn and Adiu are seated, looking through papers in front of them. He bows to them, and they rise, bowing in return. The afternoon discussion concerns *The No Fir* (the Book of Wisdom) and its application to the proposed partnership. Aeat is unprepared. He thought he would have more time. Qyn addresses Aeat's questions directly with passages from *The No Fir*. Adiu writes more than she had in the morning, referencing passages and explaining her thoughts and ideas before asking questions. This information gives Aeat significant insight into her beliefs and, more importantly, Adiu. A chime signals the Evening Meal. Adiu rises, bows, and departs. Aeat pushes in all the chairs. Qyn waits for him. Once in the hallway, she summons him to her office.

Qyn says, "We know you are unprepared for all the information you received today. Just like you, Adiu has received a copy of our research. She and I have spoken in great detail about her concerns. Neither of us believes you are not a good match. But understand there are some areas you will need to show growth. I imagine you have some places for her as well. Adiu asked me to give you this. It is a City Speak translation of *The No Fir*. She also requests an additional day of meetings before you depart. If possible, with such short notice. Adiu understands that you may not be able to do so. Stay at my family's homestead if you are able. The telephone in my meeting room is at your disposal."

Qyn knocks on the meeting room door. After telling her he cannot remain, they bow, and she leaves the room.

***

Aeat picks up his belongings and follows a staff member who will take him to the train station. After leaving Qyn's office, the first thought that crosses Jotre's mind is Adiu: Displaying her heritage in such a manner, trying to prove her superiority. All the formality and dressing well beyond her means. She is just a "digger".

Jotre changes and packs his clothing in the gentlemen's bathroom at the train station. He buys a sandwich and a boxed drink at the deli counter. Jotre finishes paying just as his train arrives.

Settling into his shared third-class compartment, Jotre begins reading *The No Fir*.

"Sir, we are ten minutes out," the train conductor informs him after knocking and opening his compartment door. Jotre jolts awake.

***

In the following days, Jotre divides his time between the needs of his customers, his family, and his study of *The No Fir*. He finds the book fascinating. Although not sold on it as a book of wisdom, Jotre begins to see why the homesteaders may take it as such. Correspondence with Qyn concerns overall concepts and specific passages. Adiu responses are shared as well. Jotre checks out several volumes of government-approved historical publications from a River Bend city library to provide a counter view. One book directly talks about the Diggers:

"Those who choose to continue the "old ways" are ignorant to the point of being backward. Their book of wisdom, The No Fir, *old speak for Know First, was handed to the first thirteen couples and created as a life manual for all generations. Monotheism (One Deity) and one book for twenty-six people and their descendants are absurd. Every other old-time religion limited itself to just one.*

As the orthodox ideals and practices began to lose favor with believers in all other religions, amendments and substitutions occurred. With a desire for better lives in city and town society, many homesteaders no longer saw the need for archaic practices such as religion and individualism.

On Beta, the second planet, the invention of the assembly line changed life forever. Production becomes more efficient because each worker performs only one task instead of completing the entire job. With their focus undivided, each person's productivity exponentially increased. The raw material to the finished product time equally decreased. It was a win for the owner and employee. As the owner's expenses reduced, the employee wages and benefits increased. Owners provided their workers with wages that allowed them to purchase their products. More consumers with monetary means to buy new and better items benefited society. All are prosperous except the orthodox gatherers.

This plant-based group consists of the children and grandchildren of the "Diggers", a name given to those living outside modern society who follow the old ways because they dig into hills and mountains for shelter and the ground for food. *Their book* The No Fir states that the land and its resources belong to all people and are owned by none. They do not resist when modern society takes from them. They move on.

The contemporary government removed the Diggers from Alfa, the first planet, and placed them on Beta when its resources became limited and interplanetary space travel became possible. The Great Schism (The Great Divide) was modern society's final solution to its Digger problem. The Beta Planetary Government ordered all people outside the city or towns to be transported to the thirteenth and last planet in the solar system. They had one Beta year to report. The Beta planetary government transported them by train and shuttle to the closest city with an interplanetary docking station. Thus began their long journey by contracting commercial and private spaceships.

Upon arrival, the Diggers understand why the Beta Planetary government chose their new home. Except for a large dome, the land above ground is void of life. Underground tunnels lead in every direction, and stalls with animals and homesteading equipment fill alcoves. After checking in, a travel agent directs each family into a large room. A presentation begins by explaining the services they will receive. Based on its size, each family receives a book of coupons redeemable for materials and animals to assist in their transition.

They were also assigned a homestead and a wagon filled with essential maintenance items. Their first responsibility is getting their assigned draft animals from the nooks and returning them to their designated wagon. A person assigned to their family assists them in harnessing the animals and collecting the items inside their coupon book. A rider and horse lead the family to their new home.

The Beta Planetary Government explored and colonized the remaining ten planets throughout the following generations. The Industrial Complex expanded its reach and advancements based on its origin: The Assembly Line.

*** See The Beta Planetary Government Proclamations ***

The Beta Planetary Government "Great Schism" Proclamation

It has come to the attention of the Beta Planetary Government council members a "Great Schism" has formed between our modern society within the city and town citizens and those citizens who choose to reside in faraway communities and villages.

There has always been a significant separation between these two groups ideologically, ethically, and geographically. The choice to live outside the comfort, convenience, and security of Modern Society has remained the option exercised by the second group for generations. They view the freedom to practice their archaic religious beliefs, non-genetically modified foods, and their freedom to migrate for their nutritionally and shelter needs worthy for exile from Modern Society.

The Modern Society no longer desires to worship unseen deities scientifically proven to not exist, depend on the whims of nature to feed them, and the inconvenience of relocating when there exists the advantages of available property ownership and industrialization without the excessive manual expenditures required by all other political, religious, and communal options.

To ensure the proper and uniform utilization of Planet Beta's limited resource by all of its citizenry, the Beta Planetary Government council has passed by committee and resolution the following proclamations:

1. The Beta Planetary Government shall oversee all of its citizens' activities to ensure their uniform compliance to the societal norms, mandates, and laws as set forth by its ruling body members. In exchange for a citizen's adherence, they shall receive an equal portion of The Beta Planetary Office of Citizen Financial Subsidy (BPOCFS) support provided by the Beta Planetary Government as designated by its council members. This portion shall be of such an amount as to allow the citizen to live a life without need.

2. The Beta Planetary Government shall oversee all of its citizens' medical needs to ensure their compliance to the societal norms and mandates as set forth by its ruling body members concerning their emotional, medical and physical needs. In exchange for a citizen's adherence, they shall receive free care through The Beta Planetary Office of Citizen Health Services (BPOCHS) as designated by its council members. These health services shall be available in equal measure. There will be an opportunity for citizens to use their individual fund for supplemental care.

3. The Beta Planetary Government shall oversee all of its citizens' transportation needs to ensure their compliance with environmental and societal mandates and laws as set forth by its ruling body members. In exchange for a citizen's exclusive use of the provided transportation services, they shall receive these without cost through a planetary government controlled business entities in each city and town through The Beta Planetary Office of Citizen Transportation (BPOCT) as designated by its council members. These transportation services shall be available in equal measure. There will be an opportunity for citizens to use their individual funds for upgraded or supplemental services.

4. The Beta Planetary Government shall oversee all of its' businesses' geographical locations to ensure their services are equally available to all citizens' needs. In exchange for a business' location compliance, its owners shall receive the financial advantages of providing their services to a designated number of citizens without the need to compete with other local similar businesses. These independent business entities' activities shall be controlled by The Beta Planetary Office of Business Affairs (BPOBA) as designated by its council members to ensure all citizens have uniform business service opportunities within a designated geographical location. There will be an opportunity for citizens to use their individual funds for supplemental services.

5. The Beta Planetary Government shall oversee all news and media outlets' activities to ensure their compliance with societal norms, mandates and laws as set forth by its governing body concerning the reporting of factual representations of individual citizens, organizations and governmental agencies. In exchange for their compliance, they will be provided an equal portion of The Beta Planetary Office of Media Financial Subsidy (BPOMFS) support provided by The Beta Planetary Government as designated by their council members. This portion shall be of such an amount as to allow the news and media outlets to financially meet their not only their needs but most of their wants.

6. The Beta Planetary Government shall abolish all religious practices and beliefs, as they are archaic and unnecessary. A Modern Society has been built on its citizens' logical and critical thinking ability to learn and apply proven scientific truths without the permission or assistance of unseen deities. All religious buildings will be demolished and replaced with scientific academic institutions to be utilized by its citizens for the enrichment of individual and group achievement and Beta's Planetary society as well.

As presented, these proclamations provide individual citizens, business and private organizations and the Beta Planetary society as a whole the opportunity to enjoy success and prosperity. The only Beta Planetary Government requirement for its citizens is to sign The Beta Planetary Government Pledge of Compliance (BPGPC) at their local municipal government building by the end of six Beta calendar months.

Those citizens who choose not the sign The Beta Planetary Government Pledge of Compliance Pledge (BPGPC) within six Beta calendar months will forfeit the chance to do so, and will be left with only two choices: 1. Loss of all personal possessions and relocation into a Beta Planetary Government Rehabilitation Program and to remain until deemed a productive member of society or 2. Retention of personal possessions and participation in The Beta Planetary Government Relocation Program (BPGRP) on Planet Nu, the thirteenth and last planet in our galaxy.

Participants and their possessions in the Beta Planetary Government Relocation Program (BPGRP) will be transported from the nearest shuttle station to Beta Planetary Government bound trains, where they will have themselves and their possessions transferred to the appropriate trains, and finally to Beta Planetary Government approved government, commercial, and individual owned space transport. Upon arrival, these citizens will check in with the Beta-Nu Planetary Relocation Transportation Program (BNPRTP) personnel who will assign their space craft.

Upon arrival at The Nu Planetary Office of Relocation Program (NPORP) station, each family or individual Nu citizen will register their arrival. In exchange for participation in The Beta Planetary Government Relocation Program (BPGRP), each Nu citizen will receive new citizen documentation and participate in an orientation presentation. Completion of these steps will result in a coupon book containing coupons to be used at various Nu Government approved mercantile located in The Nu Planetary Office of Relocation Program (NPORP) station, and drivers to assist with the collection of these items and to drive your horse-drawn wagon to your assigned underground homestead. All these are provided free of charge by The Beta Planetary Government Relocation Program (BPGRP) support designated by The Beta Planetary Government council members.

The Beta Planetary Government Council

Chapter 4

Mara's & Jotre's Journey Begins
Fourteenth Day, Fourth Month, 2159

In the parlor, Jotre gathers his clothes to pack while Mara walks around her suite. Her luggage sits next to the front door. Four shiny metal trunks of various sizes are piled upon one another, with her toiletry bag adorning its pinnacle. Jotre carries his garment bags and a large leather suitcase over. With these additions, the perimeter of the pile increases in width, thus making a hill into a mountain. Just then, a telephone in the parlor rings.

"Mrs. Mara Ana Hener, the driver you requested, has arrived. Should I send him?" the concierge at the front desk inquires.

"Yes, of course. Also, two porters and rolling carts with hooks for … one, two, and three garment bags. Make that three porters. One for my toiletry and traveling bags. I cannot handle more than my handbag and fan today."

Turning her right wrist to read the numbers on her gem-encrusted watch, Mara says, "Inform the driver we are CLOSE to being late for our arrival time at the River Bend central train station and the porters to be their MOST EFFICIENT as well. If OUR train leaves without us aboard, I shall NEVER forgive them. And YOU and the APARTMENT MANAGEMENT as well! Chop! Chop!" Jotre takes the handset, placing it down gently in its receiver.

When these last statements come through the switchboard wires, the driver and porters are already on Mara's floor. Eavesdropping on the conversation, a switchboard operator clasps both hands over her mouth to muffle the pain from the ringing in her ears. The more experienced concierge had covered the earpiece of his handset with his hand before making the call.

"Mother, please calm down. One of the specific reasons you chose this apartment complex is its reputation for excellent service. Have they ever not met or exceeded your expectations?" Jotre hugs her from behind.

"You are right. But I don't want today to be the exception. You know how much I detest those who think the entire universe revolves around them and everyone else should wait." He releases her, and she turns to give him a light kiss. The knocker drops back into place with a thud.

Instructing the porters and driver, Mara says, "Everything is there; hang the garment bags on the passenger side hooks. They shouldn't be moving around everywhere, getting wrinkles in them. You will place my toiletry bag on the floor of the front seat. It must remain upright, or everything will spill." Mara straightens her back, lifting her chin to look down past her nose at the driver. She extends herself to all six feet of her height and grabs her miniature handbag and fan.

Mara and Jotre enter the lobby just as the bells of the two service elevators ring. The doorman, looking smart in his embroidered three-piece suit and cap, is waiting patiently. The driver strides quickly and opens the trunk. Jotre reaches for his mother's elbow, escorting her forward.

Mara continues her directions until all the pieces are correctly loaded and tied down. Jotre waits for his mother at the driver's side rear door.

"Don't you dare take the long way! You will receive enough of a tip! It is best to go through the city at this time of day. I will tell you the way."

While Mara's monologue continues, Jotre sits back, thinking and trying to relax. Anyone who doesn't know my family well would be surprised to learn they come from "Diggers." Father refused to stay underground. He executed his escape by attending a secondary school in a distant city. Not a First Born, to whom this choice would have been acceptable, Father was the youngest, expected to stay on the homestead, care for his parents, and pass it on to his youngest child when he died. But Father was having none of it. Uncle Efram, his older brother, owned a homestead near their parents and enjoyed the life. After Secondary School, Father interned with an electrical engineering firm that provided services to the city of River Bend. It seemed strange that he married not one but two "digger" women. But then his second wife, Mara, was twenty-six years his junior and adored him.

The vehicle stops in the Porter Area of the above-ground River Bend train station entrance. Jotre jumps out his door, racing to his mother's door to open it as she sits, tapping her fingers on the back of the driver's seat. A train station porter opens the trunk, sees the number and size of trunks, and calls for assistance.

Jotre closes the door upon his mother's departure and walks forward to care for the driver. He sees the driver exhale slowly.

"Do not forget my toiletry bag! Nothing better be spilled!" comes from the back as Mara directs the train station porters in their duties. A smile crosses Jotre's lips as he completes the transaction with the driver and gives him a generous tip.

***

Jotre is waiting in the will-call line for their tickets. He sends a silent prayer upward for the few passengers ahead of him. The ticket counter agent efficiently provides each individual or group with their tickets and information about their trip, including the train's expected departure time, track number, side of the track the train will be on, the number of their carriage, and seat numbers. He asks if there are any questions, then calls for the next in line as each leaves.

When Jotre's turn comes, the ticket agent says, "Your identification card, please."

"Here you are," as Jotre removes it from the right inside pocket of his suit.

"These are the first-class tickets for Mrs. Mara Ana Hener and Mr. Jotre Jotu Mara on Train #13, the River Bend - Lake Ephrata Express, on Track #13 on the left side of Platform #7. You have been assigned Carriage #13. It is the first First-Class carriage after the Second-Class carriages with platform side individual doors. As promised, you and Mrs. Mara Ana Hener have the seats nearest the front of the carriage. The special services you have requested have been added to this personalized itinerary," presenting the two tickets, itinerary, and a list of services available during their journey.

Seeing Jotre, Mara states, "I will follow you to the baggage car to ensure you handle my delicate trunks and their contents appropriately. You do know what I mean by appropriately, do you not?"

"No, you won't, Mother. I will take care of everything from here. You know how tired you get walking so far; you may need to rest a few times before arriving at our carriage. Our train is number thirteen on the left side of platform number seven. Our carriage is also number thirteen, the last of the first-class cars. We have two seats in the front. When our tickets were booked, I asked for the front seats because they had the most legroom. I will be along shortly. You may board as soon as you arrive," says Jotre. If the train station porters feel relief at this turn of events, they try hard not to show it.

Ticket #1: River Bend - Lake Ephrata Express
Departure 4:45, Arrival 10:56
Traveler: Mrs. Mara Ana Hener
First Class, Carriage Number 13, Seat Number 2

Ticket #2: River Bend - Lake Ephrata Express
Departure 4:45, Arrival 10:56
: Mr. Jotre Jotu Mara
First Class, Carriage Number 13, Seat Number 1

Personalized Itinerary - Special Services
Premium Tea Service
Gentlemen's Dressing Room w/Attendant
Ladies' Dressing Room w/Attendant

"Let us go forth, gentlemen; our mission requires our utmost attention and diligence," Jotre says, pointing his walking cane toward their destination—the small troop moves forward, with Jotre capturing his mother's right arm at the elbow. She matches him stride for stride, back straight, and chin up. A red glow forms on Mara's face, but she refuses to stop or rest until safely dispatched to her seat. Jotre monetarily ensures that all the trunks arrive in their present condition.

As the train whistle blows, Jotre boards the train and prepares to enter their carriage. Mara's voice echoes into the vestibule, each word bouncing off its walls—another prayer for patience before he pulls back the door.

With vigorous shaking of her large, black silk and ribbon fan, Mara is talking loudly to the people near her, "My Jotu worked so hard when he was alive to make sure that my every need and want was taken care of and is still. Jotu was so well educated that he left secondary school with three different engineering degrees; he was the first student to get an internship and the first intern hired directly. Jotu's employers were so impressed that he was

39

the fastest person at their firm to move through the ranks in its history and the first to be selected by the government to work on their latest projects. And I am not talking about the River Bend government; that was Jotu's first job. I am speaking of the NEXT for THE Universal Alliance government. The Twelve Colonial Governments consolidated, and the Universal Alliance government was in its infancy. Jotu's work was instrumental in the high quality and longevity we enjoy today and many more years to come, and his work was so secretive that Jotu had to sign a nondisclosure agreement. Oops, maybe I should not have said that last part," and giggles.

"Mother, after such a long ordeal, you must be ready for something to drink and eat. I know I am. Would you like a drinks menu? I will send a carriage attendant to take your order," Jotre says.

Within a moment, the attendant appears over Mara's shoulder. Jotre hands him the individualized itinerary. After reading its contents, an open menu the size of a children's picture book is placed in her hands. Jotre lowers himself into the seat next to Mara after putting his top hat on his walking stick and both into the corner.

Warm, thick towels are offered with golden tongs from a heated metal box. After each set of hands are washed, the towels are returned. Oval tables appear before each carriage occupant, and a formal tea table setting commences.

Pristine white runners, golden napkins decorative lunch ware, imprinted chargers and plates, and polished crystal glasses.

Premium Tea Service
Sliced, Raw & Fermented Vegetables
Cured & Raw Cold Meats and Fish
Complementary Cheeses and Spreads
Regional Specialty Crackers & Toasted Breads
Filled Pastries & Finger Sandwiches
Fried Meat, Grain & Vegetable Rolls
Chef Selected Dessert Tray

A top-shelf whiskey sour, unsweetened iced tea, and afternoon tea platters shortly arrive at Mara's and Jotre's tables. The platters are filled to their edges with genetically modified food of the highest standards.

Circular tubes arch-shaped above the table tops rise slightly to hold the glassware and plates in place. Traveling in a vacuum and hovering above the ground, the train moves smoothly through the tunnels and stations. As an express train, it will only stop once it reaches its destination. Platters such as theirs, varying in size, quantities, and selection of items, are found upon most of the tables within the first-class carriage. Mara and Jotre eat in silence until the dessert tray rolls toward them.

Mara signals for the attendant and whispers something in his ear. He cocks his head to the side, thinks for a moment, and is off. The carriage attendant returns with many small boxes and several large bags.

"It would be such a shame not to share our bounty with those who have never seen or eaten such delicacies, especially those whose hospitality we infringe upon," Mara says, selecting several desserts from the tray and indicating that the attendant should add them to the other boxes of food.

A few of the other passengers' giggles and sighs are heard. Mara snaps her head around quickly, her eyes piercing. Fans and newspapers snap into place. Jotre chuckles softly.

***

Jotre's mind wanders to the past as his mother's snoring plays in the background. *My mother* — What can I expect her behavior to be once our journey has ended and the reason for it begins? She knows how to act appropriately in society. Father paid for academic tutors, cotillion lessons, and home service provider management studies during their engagement. After Mother's final year of secondary school, she was presented as a single young lady of good breeding during the ball season and as an engaged woman during the following cotillion season. After their marriage, Mother received visitors regularly and was invited to many afternoon teas, card game nights, and even vacations at others' second homes.

But once Father passed on at seventy-two and Mother's time of mourning was over, she was lost on her own. Acceptance of Mother's invitations to and from upper-class social members decreased exponentially annually until they were only from members of her bridge club and other widows. Mother took each slight personally and became ever increasingly embittered.

Mother's financial security dwindled as well. During a market recovery, I sold her condominium in a gentile neighborhood for over three times what my parents paid. I found the rent-controlled senior living apartment where she resides. Mother believes paying rent at the upper end of the scale allows her to wreak havoc on the staff. My brother and I are also most generous when she is cruel or out of line. Mother IS sixty-eight, in the last years of her expected lifetime as a city dweller. Well, we shall see what we shall see, thinks Jotre.

Chapter 5

Mara's and Jotre's Final Preparations
Fourteenth Day, Fourth Month, 2159

A gentle alarm buzzes from Jotre's pocket watch. Getting up, he stretches the kinks out of his body. The carriage attendant arrives with a large garment bag and ushers Jotre towards the gentlemen's dressing room at the rear of the carriage. When Jotre made the trip arrangements, he was still determining if he could complete this exchange of clothes on the train. However, the voice on the other end of the telephone line assured Jotre that not only was this possible, but there would also be a room set aside, and it would have an attendant just for him.

The well-attired attendant sends Jotre behind a room separator and demands that he hands the attendant his clothes as Jotre removes them. Off with the short, black business jacket, buttoned vest, gold tie with its initialed clip, and white dress shirt with lapels. Next, the bottom half, leather belt, shoes, trousers, and socks.

The attendant summons Jotre from behind the divider and puts him in a clean gold silk robe and a comfortable chair beside a man's dressing table. The sound of water and the sight of steam greet Jotre next.

A few minutes later, the attendant leads Jotre to his shower around the corner of the room. From outside the curtain, a hand thrusts before him with each item as needed, removing unnecessary items. Jotre recognizes the names of the brands on the bottles from the High Street in River Bend.

With a clearing of his throat, the attendant asks, "Is Mr. Jotre Jotu Mara prepared to leave the shower?"

Upon Jotre's positive response, a hand with another gold robe appears. Opening the shower curtain, a pair of gold slippers lay on the floor before him.

The attendant opens a mirrored cabinet above the dressing table to reveal many shaving creams, hair tonics, and aftershaves. Jotre sits in the chair covered with large, soft towels. After turning him away from the mirror, the attendant lowers and leans Jotre back.

"Do you have a preference for aftershaves, Mr. Jotre Jotu Mara?"

Jotre replies, "I will leave that to your discretion if it is not a problem."

"No problem at all, sir! Am I understanding that the Matron Family Services' staff will greet you?" Jotre nods. "Then a light scent is in order. I am thinking a musk." The attendant takes the dual-sided razor in hand, beginning the shaving process.

Clean-faced and with aftershave applied, the attendant spins Jotre's chair around. "How would you like your hair dressed?"

Jotre takes a moment to think. "Straight back, part in the middle, and hair tonic to keep it in place."

"Hands off me, girl! I have suffered enough! I am returning to my seat and having a cocktail to calm my nerves before we arrive."

Jotre knows that voice. Mara has finished freshening up. Without a word, the attendant quickly removes the white starched shirt with a stand-up collar from the garment bag. With an efficiency Jotre had not witnessed previously, his buttoned shirt receives its covers and cuff links, trousers and belt are fastened, Jotre is hustled into his emerald paisley patterned vest, and his ribbon tie lays flat against his collar in a perfect bow. The attendant holds his dark green tail jacket. Jotre slides his black-gloved right hand into its sleeve and turns for his left to do the same. Jotre's brushed black top hat, which has a matching veil, makes its way to sit firmly on his head. With a final look and minor adjustments, Jotre tips the attendant and thanks him for such good service. The time has come to return to his seat.

Planning for a barrage of angry words, to his surprise, Jotre finds Mara sitting calmly in her chair, drinking coffee. His lips send gratitude upward, and he mouths a "thank you" to the carriage attendant over her head. In return, Jotre receives a slight smile.

***

Arriving at their destination, Matron Qyn's staff whisks them away. Mara goes to the best hotel in the city. Her trunks and personal items are carried directly to the Penthouse suite, unloaded, hung on padded hangers, or placed upon the shelves of the walk-in closet.

An attendant from the hotel assists Mara with her coat, hat, and gloves, then leads her to a fainting couch with three tiers of goodies and all the items required for proper tea services sitting upon a low table within arm's reach. The attendant lifts Mara's feet to lie on a silk pillow at its foot end. As she is lying back, a large neck pillow lands against the padded headrest, directly at the base of Mara's head.

"Mrs. Mara Ana Hener, my name is Jame. I will be your attendant and available during your stay. Please ring the bell at any time. I will place it on the table. What beverage may I get for you?

Which item on the table would you like as a starter?" With each response, Jame checks how to prepare it and inquires how she may serve Mara next.

Jotre and the others forgotten; they take their leave quietly. In the lobby, one of Qyn's staff members gives instructions about Mara's schedule and makes transportation arrangements with the front desk.

"Do you wish to have a meal or a drink before we leave, Mr. Jotre Jotu Mara? No alcohol is available on the Matron family's homestead," says a staff member's voice.

Although Jotre could use one or three drinks, keeping Qyn's staff waiting longer seems disrespectful. "Thank you for the offer, but I will decline. The journey has been eventful, and I am growing tired." Jotre glances back.

"Do not worry, sir. Mrs. Mara Ana Hener will receive the highest level of care," a voice comes from the group.

***

The staff walks before Jotre, opens doors, and gives him a hand into a four-wheeled horse-drawn coach. Qyn offered Jotre a room at her family homestead. This will allow them to talk outside her office, and he can see what a homestead looks like. Jotre's garment bags hang inside, and his travel bag is across from him on the seat. A young boy jumps into the driver's seat. The remainder of the staff leaves in various directions. The carriage has beautiful, if not new, tapestries and seat covers.

Jotre awakes with a start when the boy shakes him from the open door. He is unsure how long the ride is, but the world around him is dark, and the air is clear and calm. Qyn exits a bamboo and clay-tiled house, spilling candlelight onto the lush, short grasses of the rice field.

"Greetings, Aeat! Wyl tells me that Mrs. Mara Ana Hener is settled in. I hope Fir On has blessed you with an enjoyable journey and my staff has made you feel welcome."

"Too welcomed on Mother's part," Jotre says before thinking. A deep red blush comes to his cheeks.

"Let us see if we can do that for you as well," Qyn says, taking Jotre's elbow and patting his lower arm with her other hand.

The house is divided into sections with sliding resin and rice paper doors. Qyn leads Jotre to his room and tells him about the different rooms and tomorrow's agenda.

"Four generations of Matrons live on the homestead. Each family has their own house. Everyone shares the work and harvest. The Matrons give the money they earn to their family. The cavern has been increased in size as the need arose. Now it is over an acre. Our families save room by sheltering all our animals together by type. There are barns designated for each grain, fruit, or vegetable type. Each home has a root cellar, where the family's allotted food is stored. These are also used as shelters in an emergency."

Qyn and Jotre arrive at a door toward the back of the house. He sees a single sleeping pad on the floor, a small wardrobe, and a dressing table. A water pitcher, a bowl, and a chamber pot occupy the far corner. Jotre's travel bag sits on top of a chest at the foot end of the bed. Quickly undressing, he slides under the covers.

Chapter 6

Jotre Meets Equo and Iuot
Sixteenth Day, Fourth Month, 2159

Adiu and Jotre meet three more times to finalize the partnership contract's specifics. The final step before the ceremony requires receiving the blessing from the other's parents. Adiu's parents meet with Jotre after the morning meal the next day. Equo and Iuot only understand their ancestral tongue, which makes Qyn's role as a translator crucial in this meeting.

Equo and Iuot are seated across the table when Jotre enters. He is shocked. Neither wears a hat, a veil, gloves, or fancy clothes. What does this mean? Are her parents too poor to afford these things? Doesn't Adiu think he will notice the difference? How will she explain this? Is this why the parent meeting happens right before the ceremony? So there is no time to change my mind?

Jotre removes his top hat, which has its veil, and places it upside down on the table. He then removes his gloves, placing the veil inside and laying his gloves across the top.

When Jotre turns around to face the couple, Equo reaches across the table for a handshake, and then Iuot does the same. Qyn remains in her chair. She introduces Equo first and then Iuot, pronouncing each name slowly. Jotre tries pronouncing each, bringing smiles to the couple's faces. Equo says something to Qyn in the ancestral tongue.

Qyn says, "You may address them as EQ and IU. She wants to know how you would like them to address you."

Knowing that his answer will determine the course of the meeting, Jotre responds, "Aeat". Once again, Equo and Iuot smile.

"What type of work do you do, Aeat?" Iuot asks.

Aeat replies, "I repair machinery for homesteaders and townsfolk."

"Do you enjoy your work?" inquires Iuot.

Aeat says, "Yes. I like figuring out what is wrong and putting them back together after they are fixed."

"Is this what you studied at Secondary School?" asks Iuot.

Aeat says, "Yes, and agriculture. I like to grow heritage vegetables. My aunt and her husband live on a homestead. They gave me heritage seeds. The vegetables I grow are not as pretty as those grown for the city and town, but they taste much better."

The Equo and Iuot nod in unison when they hear this.

Then Iuot speaks to Qyn for a long time. A serious look comes across her face.

A series of questions flood Aeat's mind: Have I said something wrong? Are they offended? What type of questions is Iuot asking? How will I answer them? The list in his mind grows while Qyn listens to Iuot.

Finally, Qyn speaks. "If you are happy with your work and where you live, why are you asking to be partnered with someone like Adiu? Women living near you share more in common. Do you understand all you will be leaving behind? Also, your responsibilities as Adiu's partner? She does not believe in broken partnerships for any reason other than death. Adiu's homestead is at its beginning stage. It will require a great deal of planning and construction. Things will not always go according to plan. Are you willing to do what it takes to make it successful? Adiu is a determined woman who has worked hard since she was a little girl. Based on her test scores, she went to Secondary School two years early."

Qyn presents Aeat with a document:

Redsvil Secondary School
is proud to present

Adiu Equo Iuot

A Secondary Degree Certification
in General Studies with Highest Honors
Earning a Grade Average of
One Hundred Sixty Points

With Academic Pursuits in the Fields of:
*Accounting * Animal Husbandry * Biology * Botany*
*Chemistry * Construction * Finance*
Farm Machinery Maintenance & Repair
*Heritage Farming * Home Economics*
& Welding

No wonder it took so long! This also explains her high demands, Aeat realizes.

Qyn continues, "Adiu is introverted and needs time by herself. She takes time to make decisions based on information she researches or knows from experience. Once Adiu comes to a decision, it is difficult to dissuade her. When Adiu loves, she does so entirely. But she will not throw her heart away easily. You will have to earn Adiu's love and respect."

Watching Iuot talk, Aeat realizes his tone is not a boast of a proud father but a statement of a father who expects nothing less from his daughter. He also notices something else: Iuot is speaking. In their orthodox homesteading community, the woman is usually the head of the household. Yet, Equo sits there, looking toward her husband to respond.

How did Adiu learn to be the person IU describes without EQ's guidance? Or is EQ so unimpressed by me that she feels I am unworthy of her attention? How am I to answer? Why am I doing this?

Everyone is waiting for Aeat's response. He needs to figure out how to answer.

When all else fails, tell the truth comes to Aeat's mind. Aeat begins, "I know I don't want what I have had previously. There are many reasons for my relationships with women: one or both of us were lonely or willing, and it was easier than being alone. I knew I could walk away if things became uncomfortable or too much of a burden. The women made less money, had jobs requiring less skill, and were not as smart. None of them could challenge me. Maybe I grew up or realized there is more to life. One day, I was talking to a friend who used a Matron service to find her husband. They are thrilled to be together, and as a result of their partnership meetings, Ranbo and Ole returned to their family's homesteader ways. I have learned so much. Seeing how they work together, the quality of the food they grow, and their life's purpose, I realized I wanted this for myself."

Aeat continues, "I am not worthy of your daughter's consideration. Adiu is more intelligent and knows more than I may ever know. Honestly, she has a moral compass I envy. In our meetings, Adiu mentioned nothing besides graduating from Secondary School. It is understandable if you do not give your blessing to our union. I know if I were in your position, I wouldn't." After all of this, Aeat sits back in his chair, exhausted.

Qyn takes a long time to translate his words for Equo and Iuot. She stops quite a few times. Sometimes, Equo or Iuot say something or stop her.

Are they responding? Are they asking questions? How do they feel about what they are hearing?

Aeat realizes he is squeezing his hands tightly under the table. His hands are cramping from the effort. The cramps travel to Aeat's wrists and lower arms. An energy bolt shoots into his left elbow. Aeat shakes his shoulder in response. Deep breaths: take deep breaths, his brain screams.

Aeat shoves the chair back so hard that his head smacks against the wall. Thud! Aeat's eyes cross, his ears ring, and his brain gets foggy. The others look up. He shakes his head.

Aeat chuckles. His chuckles turn into giggles, and the giggles become laughter. Then Aeat snorts.

The others smile, trying to suppress their reactions. However, they are failing in their attempts. Qyn, Equo, and Iuot join in with giggles that become unbridled laughter. Regaining his composure, Iuot hands Equo a white cotton handkerchief. She blows her nose and smiles broadly. Iuot wipes the tears from his eyes with his shirt sleeve. Qyn pulls her lace fan from her left sleeve and begins fanning herself until the red leaves her face.

Qyn rings a bell. A staff member comes into the meeting room. Qyn gives a few instructions. Within moments, two staff members return with plates, cups, saucers, a coffee pot, a teapot, sugar cubes, a chilled creamer pitcher, and a platter of finger sandwiches, cut fruit and vegetables, cheeses, and meats. As everyone is being served and eating, Aeat relaxes his body, and a friendly conversation occurs.

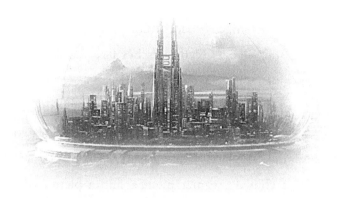

Chapter 7

Adiu awakes to the gongs of Aviqa's pendulum clock, passed down from the Firstborn daughter in her family to the next generation. It was carved from the soft wood of a felled White Pine from her first-generation grandmother's homestead on the First Planet. The last of the thirteen original couples Fir On created, Aviqa and her partner, Aviqi, were blessed with a bounty of plants to eat and forager/gatherer knowledge and skills.

It is 2:45—time to get up and prepare her morning meal. Adiu rises from under her lavender duvet and flat sheet; her feet slide into her ruby house slippers. The slippers were a gift from a friend when they graduated from Secondary School. The slippers are worn. Adiu cannot bring herself to replace them, so she replaces the needed parts and repairs the rest. The flat sheet is straightened and pulled into place. Next comes the duvet. The top fourth of the covers fold neatly toward the opposite end of Adiu's bed, and her pillow is placed and fluffed with a final pat.

It was time to pray to Fir On for her meal's bounty and life-giving energy and eat the morning meal. Several days ago, Adiu had prepared her favorite grain concoction: puffed barley, hemp hearts, pepitas (raw pumpkin seeds), and flax seeds mixed into sour yogurt, honey, and vanilla and topped off with seasonal berries, covered in milk. Without a working homestead, Adiu relies solely on her harvest portion at her parents' homestead. This situation will be changing quite soon.

Adiu will postpone her Wisdom Studies until she settles into a seat on the local shuttle. She returns to her bed chamber. While removing her sleeping garments, Adiu says a prayer of gratitude for her safety and refreshing sleep. Shaking her night clothes removes any loose dirt or dead skin, and they return to their hanger held on her wall by a single square nail.

Due to the activities for the remainder of her day, Adiu does not warm a water kettle to bathe her face and neck. Instead, the room-temperature water from a pitcher pours into a bowl in the corner near her dressing table. Just enough water splashes into the bowl to complete the job. Adiu's lips silently move in gratitude for the clean water. Feeling ready for the adventure ahead, she walks to her wardrobe, removes a set of scarlet traveling clothing, and lays each piece separately upon her bed. These garments were last worn on Adiu's journey a few days before the Winter Solstice to meet with Qyn and her parents.

Today is the day Adiu has been preparing for almost two years. She will meet Aeat's mother. Adiu lifts her chemise over her head and pulls it into place. Next, she selects her laced stay, removing the two silk laces from the eyelets in the front of the garment and laying them on her dressing table top. Adiu runs her fingers along the lines of lacy frills covering the stay for a moment, takes the laces from her dressing table, and laces herself into the garment, tightening as she goes. A blush crosses her face when Adiu looks up into the three mirrored room separator. So many thoughts are flying haphazardly through Adiu's mind. Each takes its turn, landing on her brain's nerve endings, causing pulses of energy and intense emotions, and Adiu quickly shakes her head. This is not the time now to deal with such things. Adiu must finish dressing, or she will be late. What a great impression that would make during this most critical time!

The skirt with the adjustable waist is picked up and shaken before opening it up to step inside. Adiu lines up a large rectangle to lay flat over the laces of her stay from under her bosom to its lowest part in the front. She begins tightening the laces in their eyelets, laying loosely at each hip and attached to the large rectangle and the waistband at the back of her skirt. There is one lace on each side of her dress. Starting at the bottom, Adiu moves back and forth between the two laces, ensuring they lay flat and tightened correctly. All that remains for the skirt is tying the laces on the front waistband behind her back and over the flat waistband in the back. At this point, Adiu sits on her bed to ensure that all the layers stay tight enough to be that way for the rest of the day. She reaches across her bed for her stockings. As Adiu bends each leg at the knee, her skirt and chemise fall into her lap, revealing her naked foot, ankle, and lower leg. The stocking feels cool and soft against her skin. Placing her hands on both sides of the edge of her bed, her palms facing down, and her fingers hanging over, Adiu pushes herself up to a standing position. It is not the most graceful of actions, but it is not a full catapult motion. Adiu twirls around in front of the mirrors, checking that her hems are level. Just right! Adiu's blouse is the last of the inner garments. Its scarlet ribbon running through the silk lace contrasts with but compliments the hue of the scarlet silk fabric underneath. Adiu folds back the center front panel to reveal two columns of eyelets and removes the two laces holding it together. This time, the lacing begins in the middle of two rows of eyelets, and each works in opposite directions: one toward her bosom and the other toward the floor. Taking the left edge of the center front panel in her right hand, Adiu pulls it to the left. Securing it in place, she fastens two hooks near the left edge at the top and bottom into their catches on the backside of the center front panel.

Finally, Adiu is ready for outerwear, removing a pair of black gloves from the top drawer of her dressing table; she rubs the material against her left cheek and inhales the scent of the powder sprinkled inside them after the last time Adiu wore them. The left glove first and then the right. Separating her fingers and interlacing them pushes the gloves gently into their proper position. Adiu removes her dark leather travel coat from its hook on the wall. Its lining displays a series of outdoor scenes adorned with one of a different planetary season on each of its four panels. These scenes are taken from *The No Fir* and represent the First Planet (Pla 1 in the ancestral tongue) before the Age of the Assembly Line. Adiu knows that *The No Fir* is this age's only written or oral non-governmental approved record of this time.

Looking from left to right, the first panel shows Spring (Rebi), the time of rebirth. Tiny buds are growing on the trees and plants in the short grass. The left center panel depicts Summer (Gro), the time of growth. The trees and plants have small fruit, leaves, and vegetables. Small animals play in the taller grasses and reeds. The right center panel represents Autumn (Harv). The fruit and vegetables are ready to be picked. The animals have grown larger and appear in pairs with their young. The grasses and reeds sway in the breeze. The right panel shows Winter (Dorm). It is the time of rest. The trees are bare, and the plants, grasses, and reeds are hidden away.

Adiu takes the time to pray to Fir On for the protection and warmth this coat provides and for reminding her of a time that was. Adiu's short, blond hair is brushed and placed inside a tightly crocheted snood. A black covering comes up from under her snood to cover it, and its band tightens around her head, covering her ears. Long hair pins slide into her hair and on top of her covering to hold everything down.

Adiu pulls her gloved hands and arms into the coat's sleeves and buttons the coat up the front. Lifting the back of her covering with one hand, Adiu's other hand reaches for her dark leather hat with a large circular brim and veil from its nail on the wall. Leading her hat toward the back of her head and downward to lay the bundle in her other hand inside, her veil falls below her shoulders over Adiu's coat. A hat pin runs through the top of the hat, into Adiu's covering and hair, and back out—time to pick up her suitcase and leave.

Chapter 8

The next day, Adiu and Matron Qyn sit at the table in the same meeting room where Aeat and her parents met. The door opens, and Mara comes bustling in. The ladies stand up.

"I know I am late. It just can't be helped. Jame, my hotel assistant, took her sweet time this morning. Then, the hotel restaurant messed up my breakfast order, the exact order I have every morning," she says.

Then Mara looks at Qyn and Adiu. They bow, and she returns the favor. Mara stares at Adiu. Today, she wears an emerald green outfit similar to her scarlet one, complete with her hat, veil, and gloves.

The Matron explains, "Questions and responses are written on the paper laid before you and given to me to read. Adiu will also write her answers or questions on other sheets of paper."

Mara opens her mouth to say something, thinks better of it, and grabs the pen to begin writing. Her large writing sprawls across the multiple sheets, both front and back. While waiting for her arrival, Adiu had written several questions. So she patiently waits for Mara to finish. She gathers the sheets nearly an hour later and hands them to the Matron.

As the Matron reads through her papers, Mara says, "This method will take too long. A simple yes or no will suffice. If follow-up questions or responses are needed, they will wait until the end."

Both women look toward Adiu for a response. She nods her head once.

The Matron says, "Adiu accepts your request."

"Is she aware of our family's proud heritage? My husband, Jotu, left behind the old ways, pioneering the modern age of industry," Mara says.

The Matron answers, "She is aware."

"Does she know that Jotre is a successful entrepreneur following in his father's footsteps?" Mara asks.

The Matron responds, "She does know."

"Does she know she will be leaving her family and living in Jotre's home above ground in town?" Mara asks.

The Matron corrects Mara: "She will leave her family homestead. Adiu and Aeat will be moving to her homestead underground."

"What!" Mara says.

The Matron says, "Jotre will live outside the domes as a homesteader. He will use his inheritance as a firstborn child to supply animals and machinery. This has been agreed on and mandated as part of the partnership contract."

"Where is this partnership contract? I want to see it," Mara asks.

The Matron slides a copy of the contract to Mara. Her lips move, and her cheeks become redder as she reads it. Mara's hands touch the signatures.

Visibly shaken, Mara requests a glass of water. Qyn understands her distress and fills a crystal glass with ice and water. Mara accepts it, her hands trembling. As Qyn refills the glass, she gently rubs Mara's back.

Qyn says, "I understand your confusion. Adiu and I assumed that Jotre discussed the contents of the contract with you. We now know that is not the case. I apologize for the discomfort this situation has caused you. Would you like to return to your hotel for further review? You may contact me directly with any questions. There is still time. The final parental meeting will be just before tomorrow's union ceremony."

Gathering her composure, Mara stands up. Qyn walks with her, still rubbing her back. Adiu can hear their conversation coming from the hallway. The front door closes, and all is quiet.

***

Tears fall down her cheeks as Adiu sits back in her chair. As if in slow motion, she takes her handkerchief out of her purse, wipes her eyes, and blows her nose.

My parents are looking forward to giving Aeat their blessing tomorrow. He makes me laugh and challenges me; Adiu thinks We have worked well together on the contract and our plans for the homestead.

Qyn's sister, Lyn, also a matchmaker, knocks on the jamb of the still-open door. Adiu looks up from her chair. Lyn walks across the room and hugs her from behind. She removes the hairpin from Adiu's hat and lifts the hat and veil from her head. The covering and snood follow. Light blond hair tumbles down just above her shoulder blades. A fresh set of tears fall, and sobs fill the silence. Lyn sits beside her, taking Adiu in her arms and rocking her gently.

"Adiu, you did nothing wrong. You have studied so hard to make Aeat and his mother feel comfortable. You have shown them you respect their ways. Qyn and I know how much you spent to dress as their ancestors did. All of us were unprepared for how far away they had moved from their heritage. They do not understand. You are not like them in this way. You have given enough. It is time to show who you are. Qyn and I still believe in this partnership. I think you do, too. Don't throw Aeat away based on this meeting with his mother. He has reasons for leaving his present life and embracing a new one with you. Now, go to the bathroom and freshen up. Qyn is taking Mara Ana Hener back to her hotel. She will call Aeat so his mother's reaction will not catch him off guard. There has been enough of that for one day. I will be in the meeting room near my office when you are ready. We will have our Midday Meal and Wisdom Studies together. You may be able to assist me with a passage I do not quite understand," says Lyn.

Upon arriving at the staff room, Adiu is greeted by all the Matrons and their staff. Sharing funny stories while passing plates of homegrown food makes Adiu feel better, and the Wisdom Study strengthens her beliefs. It also reinforces Adiu's resolve to share her life with Aeat.

***

Qyn calls Aeat at her homestead to discuss the office events. Aeat thanks her for the information and says he will leave to meet with his mother.

Arriving at Mara's hotel room, Jotre knocks on the door.

Jame opens the door, steps forward, and closes it behind her.

Jame says, "The hotel doctor has been to see Mrs. Mara Ana Hener. She was hysterical, yelling and crying. The Matron and I tried to calm her down, but Mrs. Mara Ana Hener seemed to worsen. The doctor gave her some pills, but she just threw them across the room. It took four porters to hold Mrs. Mara Ana Hener down so the doctor could give her a shot. She is resting now. The doctor said Mrs. Mara Ana Hener should sleep until morning. He will return later to check on her."

Jotre blames himself. I should have shown Mother the contract and explained what I was doing earlier. I knew from experience that Mother would not be in favor of it. But I hoped that an opportunity to ride a long-distance train in first class and stay in a nice hotel would soften her. Although Mother did not understand why I had changed my attire on the train, she was willing to play along if she could return to her high society days.

Deep in his soul, Jotre knows Mara will refuse to give her blessing tomorrow. His mind races with thoughts: What happens then? Can Adiu and I still be partners? Will Adiu even want me after this? Why do I care so much? I respect and care for EQ and IU. What will they think of me? Will they also refuse their blessing?

Jotre's body begins to shake. Why does Mother need to make my life so difficult? I am not even her favorite child. Isac has always held a special place in Mother's heart. She plays on his insecurities, and Isac allows her to walk over him. He is always at her beck and call. Isac willingly participates in Mother's games, creating drama for those around them. Questions continue to plague his thoughts.

***

Adiu arrives at her apartment. Similar thoughts are swirling inside her head. The research before Adiu states that both sides of Aeat's family are homesteaders. Mara should be knowledgeable about the orthodox homesteader marriage protocols and arrangements. Did Aeat not tell her about their plans? Why would he do that? Is Aeat ashamed of me and my family? I have worked so hard to make his transition easier. I have spent a great deal of money toward a partnership that may not happen. I am not the only one. My parents gave them my share of their homestead, including significant money, equipment, and livestock. I know my parents have become quite fond of Aeat.

All Adiu can do at this moment is pray. Falling to her knees, "Fir On, I am lost in despair. So many emotions are whipping my body and cutting into my soul. I have prayed so often and so long for your guidance. Until now, I have stood steadfast in the knowledge that I followed your words and obeyed *The No Fir.* I beg you, take away my pain. Hold me in your arms so I may find peace and contentment. I seek your guidance. Help me focus my positive energy on Aeat and Mara."

***

As the Evening Meal chime sounds, Aeat makes a telephone call. Qyn will pick him up from Mara's hotel. As Qyn and Aeat travel home, she tries to offer comfort.

"Tomorrow is another day. Give your mother some time. If you end the contract with Adiu, there will be consequences, but we can work things out," Qyn says.

Aeat thinks, "Adiu exceeds my expectations as a partner, and I want to live a homestead life. Will I have to choose between Mother and my new life? I don't want to do that. I didn't expect it to be this complicated."

Qyn's voice interrupts Aeat's thoughts, "You can do nothing tonight but pray for guidance. I will sit with you and pray if you desire. Adiu and her parents will be doing the same. In dealing with people for as long as I have, I find that the right thing happens. It may take time. But in the end, it is always correct for those involved."

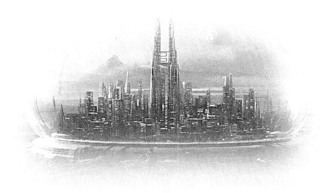

Chapter 9

Mara's Letter
Eighteenth Day, Fourth Month, 2159

A letter bearing Adiu's name arrives at the Matron Family Services' office, nestled among the early morning mail. A staff member, aware of the impending meeting after the Morning Meal, places the letter on Qyn's desk, ensuring it catches her attention upon her arrival.

As Qyn comes around her desk to see her schedule for the day, she recognizes the handwriting on the letter. Everything within her wants to tear it open and read it, but it is not addressed to her. A prayer for Adiu and Aeat ascends upward. Qyn follows it with another to grant her inner peace and wisdom. She calls a staff member into her office, emphasizing the participants' right to privacy and comfort during the meeting.

"You will take an array of beverages and a serving set to the next-door meeting room. Also, once everyone has arrived, they should be undisturbed, even if the meeting continues for the remainder of the day. The staff should slip any messages under the door. The participants in this morning's meeting will serve themselves. I will ring you directly if they need your services. You will remain on call in your office until I relieve you of this duty. You will take your meals in your office. If you must leave, you will call Matron Myn's staff to take your place while absent."

These were unusual requests but not unprecedented. The staff member assures Qyn that she understands and will follow her instructions.

***

Equo and Iuot arrive at Qyn's office first. One of her staff leads them into the meeting room and offers something to drink. They both request black coffee and a glass of water. Aeat enters the room in a simple black suit and a white collared shirt. He dons a top hat and veil. When Qyn's voice travels down the hallway, all three rise from their chairs and wait for the door to open.

Aeat's jaw falls in disbelief. Adiu walks into the room, her appearance a complete surprise. She is wearing a purple apron over a lavender short-sleeved dress and a small straw hat at a forty-five-degree angle at the back of her head. Wooden combs hold Adiu's blond locks into place above each ear. These are not the only changes: a delicate golden butterfly curves around the outermost edge of Adiu's left ear, held in place with stud earrings, one on its front foot and the other on its tail. Thirteen golden chains appear from behind her ear, just below her lobe. On each is a small inscribed medallion with two names. The outermost medallion has the names of her parents. Equo's name is above Iuot's.

Aeat realizes the others are waiting for him. A blush spreads across his face. He closes his mouth. Adiu turns, bowing to her parents and Aeat. Instinctively, he bows as well. As Aeat returns to a standing position, his eyes meet Adiu's—the air races from his body as if Aeat has received a punch to the chest. Emerald green encases black orbs. The moment breaks when Adiu reaches up and removes Aeat's top hat and veil, tossing them across the room into the corner. Giggles spills out of her, instantly changing the atmosphere. A peal of melodic, unencumbered laughter follows, filling the room with lightheartedness. Equo stares disapprovingly at Adiu. Iuot tries to contain himself, but he soon joins in. The sound is contagious. Aeat chuckles and returns to his chair.

As the silliness ends and composure returns, Qyn enters the room. Everyone stands and bows. She takes her place at the head of the table.

Qyn says, "Adiu, a letter addressed to you arrived here this morning. Would you be more comfortable taking this into another room? I can sit with you as you read it."

Something in Qyn's voice suggests to her that this is more of an order than a request. Adiu stands and slides her chair under the table. The others' faces show concern and confusion.

After being seated in Qyn's office, Adiu looks closely at the letter. At once, she recognizes the handwriting. Taking the letter opener from Qyn, Adiu inhales deeply and slides it inside the edge of the envelope. On stationary from the hotel where Mara is staying, she read the following:

Adiu Equo Iuot,

I am writing to you because we share a commonality. We are strong, firstborn women who have worked hard to get what we want. I wanted a hard-working husband who could give me the social status and advantages I desired since childhood. You have succeeded in being prepared to share your orthodox homesteading life with an equally determined partner.

Although Jotre is unaware of the significance of your attire and behavior, I appreciate the effort and cost of honoring our heritage. When Jotre appeared in traditional dress on the train, I knew it was for your sake. At that moment, I also became aware of your importance to Jotre.

Jotre has had many relationships with women, but they have kept his interest only briefly. I knew Jotre was considering utilizing the services of a matchmaker but didn't know that Jotre had done so and was looking to return to the homesteading life. In retrospect, I should have known. Jotre has not been comfortable living and working under the domes. Jotre does not have his father's competitiveness or willingness to exploit others' weaknesses. Jotre is too kind-hearted for his own good.

I have read the partnership contract. Let us get to the requirements:

1. Jotre grew up in Lebanon, a vast city with an extensive system of connected towns. It shares many towns and suburbs with its neighboring cities of Salunga and Manheim, creating a colossal network of above-ground residences and businesses. Only through other family members does Jotre experience the homesteading life. Are you willing to take the time to teach Jotre the skills he needs when you can find someone who already possesses them?

2. None of Jotre's family or friends are orthodox homesteaders. Jotre must be willing to study and learn the ancestral tongue and ways. I wonder if Jotre has the ability or fortitude to devote the necessary time and energy to such activities, even for you.

3. Are you willing to have a partner who has engaged in sexual relations with other women outside the bonds of matrimony?

4. As a firstborn, Jotre has always taken his family obligations seriously, even ending relationships with friends. Jotre has taken care of me better than any of his siblings. I know who to call first when I am in need. I will always be Jotre's first concern.

5. Jotre was in a previous relationship with an older woman. Their age difference is about the same as the two of you. She is one of my best friends. She is a lovely woman who took such good care of Jotre. Jotre led her to believe they would be married. Then, without notice, Jotre told her she needed to move out. Heartbroken, I took her into my home. When she was ready, she moved far away. I nearly lost a good friend. Have you considered that Jotre may not be mature enough to handle the struggles related to you getting older?

6. I know Jotre went to a nearby Secondary School and started working part-time at fourteen to pay for it. His father had passed away, and I could not finance Jotre's education. I only discovered Jotre had graduated when I saw Jotre's diploma on his desk while looking for a pen. Another event must have been on the same night as Jotre's graduation ceremony.

7. Jotre can be contrary when he has a mind to be. Growing up, Jotre was the first of my children to argue or disagree with my decisions. Jotre could not see the merit in taking advantage of situations for one's benefit, especially if it caused others pain or cost them financially.

8. Neither of you will ever know the blessing children can bring to your life. I have. My husband was virile and enjoyed every aspect of sexual intimacy. During Jotre's relationship with my friend, Jotre began experiencing episodes of impotence. I can only imagine the condition worsening as Jotre ages. Are you prepared to have a sexless partnership?

I like you. I do not want you to enter into a partnership that most surely will be unfulfilling and unsuccessful. You deserve so much more than a partnership with Jotre will give you.

I contacted my younger son, Isac, this morning. He tells me that Jotre has left everything behind.

By the time you read this, I will have gone. I cashed in my first-class return ticket and arranged to transport my belongings to my friend Katrina's house. I cannot return to my apartment after all the fuss made. I would be too embarrassed. Besides, they were so dreadful to me.

I also contacted my lawyer. As his mother, I can disinherit Jotre and take away his name. I have completed the paperwork to do just that. It will take effect as soon as the notary reviews and stamps it. My name is also listed as the owner of Jotre's house and personal belongings. Without his name, Jotre does not exist! He cannot touch any money in his bank accounts, own property, sign contracts, or be employed. Jotre will return to me.

Although neither of you will see it now, I have done the right thing for both of you.

Mara Ana Hener

Chapter 10

Responses to Mara's Letter
Eighteenth Day, Fourth Month, 2159

Adiu hands the letter to Qyn. She stands up and begins pacing the length of the room, turning quickly. When Adiu reaches the end, she returns to where she had just come from. Adiu stops only when Qyn stands in front of her.

Qyn says, "I know this is a sudden turn of events. Please tell me what you think—everything, even if it does not make sense."

"How could Mara do that to her son? What will he do? She has left him with nothing. What can be done to make this right?" asks Adiu. Then Adiu falls into Qyn's arms. Her head lays against her right clavicle. Qyn almost drops Adiu's limp body. Slowly, she lowers her to the floor. Qyn reaches up for a pillow to place under Adiu's head. With the assistance of her nearest desk corner, she gets up from her knees. Qyn reaches for the telephone and dials the number of her on-call staff member. Instructions are given. The staff member knocks on the door. She has a blanket and a glass of iced water in her hands. After covering Adiu with the blanket and putting the glass on the edge of Matron's desk, the staff member lowers herself onto the floor, with her back against the desk. She will remain there until Matron Qyn returns. Even though the staff member does not know the details, she can see the concern on Matron's face. She silently prays for the young woman in the room and those meeting with Matron.

Myn enters Qyn's meeting room. She leans down between Adiu's parents and begins talking to them in the ancestral tongue. Equo and Iuot stand up and push in their chairs without saying a word. They are escorted from Qyn's meeting room to Myn's at the opposite end of the hallway. The door closes behind them. Aeat is left alone.

Qyn walks in and seats herself opposite Aeat. A staff member closes the door soundlessly.

"Mara will not be joining us. She has conveyed her wishes to Adiu in the form of a letter. Under normal circumstances, I would not share its contents with you without her permission, but Adiu cannot give it now," Qyn says.

A look of concern enters Aeat's face. He is just about to speak when Qyn stops him.

Qyn continues, "Adiu will be fine. She needs time to take in everything." She hands over the pages and says, "This will be difficult to read, but you have our support."

Qyn watches as Aeat reads the letter. His face and body contort as his emotions wash across them. When Aeat is finished, the sheets fall from his fingers. He is so very pale that Qyn thinks he may also faint.

Aeat says, "Mother has done it. I always knew Mother was capable. I just never thought she would do it. Even Mother could not be that cold-hearted. How did Adiu take reading this?"

"Adiu's only concern is for you. She may have spared you the pain by releasing you from the contract. That was until Adiu read the last paragraphs. They are the only reason you are reading the letter without her permission. My sister, Myn, is explaining your situation to Equo and Iuot. They know nothing about what else is written in the letter. Please go back to my homestead. One of the staff will take you. Take some time to rest; this matter can wait. Remember, together, we will work through it," says Qyn.

Aeat is in shock. He allows Qyn to walk him to the office's front door. Two staff members take over. He is lifted into the carriage and placed on the seat. One of them sits across from him. The other drives them underground towards Qyn's homestead.

***

Myn is fielding questions when Qyn enters the room. Unable to keep up with the two conversations going at the same time, she sits down on a nearby chair and listens. Equo is irate. She is speaking so fast. Myn and Iuot try to calm her down, but their words are lost under the intensity and volume of Equo's tirade. Catching a few words here and there, Mara's upbringing and parentage are in question, with a few swear words Qyn did not think Fir On would be pleased about.

Thinking Myn and Iuot had suffered enough, Qyn clears her throat loudly and rises from her chair, "That is enough! Listen to you! Do you think Fir On is looking at you with pride? Think about Aeat. He is not Aeat anymore. He has lost his name. Equo, you know how important your name is to you. Put yourself into his place. That poor young man no longer knows who he is. He does not exist anywhere. He has lost his heritage, money, and ability to live within society. He cannot even if he wants to be Adiu's partner. And Adiu cannot enter into a partnership with him. What about Adiu's feelings?"

Equo hangs down her head. Iuot puts his arm around her back, rubbing her arm. He whispers something in Equo's ear. She smiles, nodding her head. Equo stands up and walks toward the door. Myn catches up to her in the hallway. They head to Qyn's office to see Adiu.

***

Iuot remains behind. He looks like a man with something serious on his mind.

"Equo and I have come to care for this young man. He does not deserve this treatment. We are willing to do whatever we can. We do not know what that may be," Iuot says in the ancestral tongue.

Qyn asks, "Are Equo and you positive about doing this? It could require a great deal on your part. It may mean that Adiu and he cannot be partners. How will she react if that is the case?"

"I know our daughter. Adiu wants what is best for him. I cannot imagine that Adiu would put her desires above his needs. But having said that, we need to find a way, if possible, they do not have to make such a choice," Iuot responds.

Qyn says, "Let us pray for Fir On's guidance and mercy. I believe an answer is available as long as we are willing to take the time to search for it."

When Myn and Equo arrive at Qyn's office, Adiu is lying on the peach silk sofa with a pillow behind her head, a cool towel on her forehead, and wrapped snuggly in the blanket. A cup of tea sits on the ottoman near her elbow. Adiu's eyes are closed, but she is awake. Equo races over and sits on the edge of the sofa. She lifts a spoonful of tea from the cup to Adiu's lips.

In the ancestral tongue, Equo says, "Sit up. Drink this. Such foolishness. Causing a scene. Matron Qyn's staff has better things to do than to care for a silly girl who faints over a simple thing like a letter. Now apologize."

Adiu does as she is told. "Matron Myn, I apologize for my foolish behavior. Please ask Matron Qyn and her staff to forgive me for wasting their time and energy. I forgot I am Adiu Equo Iuot and what I am capable of handling. I assure you and Qyn it will not happen again."

Adiu and Equo stand up. The teaspoon is replaced on the saucer. The blanket is folded, fluffed, and placed at the foot of the sofa. The towel is given to Qyn's staff member.

Myn leads the ladies back to the meeting room, where Iuot and Qyn are on their knees, praying. The three ladies join them on the floor. All remain in this position until the chime for Mid-day Meal rings.

Adiu and her family are led into the staff room. With the matter in Fir On's hands, there is nothing to do but wait. Equo, Iuot, and Adiu begin to relax a little. Iuot tells jokes his family has heard many times before. The staff finds them hilarious. Equo shares a recipe for red beet hard-boiled eggs with an intern. Adiu looks around the group. She thinks they will find a way. I am sure of it.

During the Wisdom Studies, Adiu sends a prayer of support for .. Fir On knows his name, even if no one else does.

End of Part One

Part Two: Adiu & Eiu

Chapter 11

Tuot's Proposal
Nineteenth Day, Fourth Month, 2159

"Get up. You have an important meeting."

He doesn't recognize the voice. What is happening? Where am I? Then, the memories of the previous day come flooding back. Why not? I don't have anything else to do.

A series of insistent knocks on his door are next. Sliding into work pants and a shirt, he says, "I am on my way." Barefoot, he grabs a pair of socks and shoes. After opening the door, Qyn's youngest son, Jyn, grabs his arm and pulls him toward the front of the house.

"You have to go now. Eomma will whip me if you aren't there by the end of the Midday Meal." Jyn pushes him toward the carriage.

"What is happening?" he asks.

Jyn replies, "Eomma didn't say. She just said you have to be at her office. If you cause her to be angry with me, I will be angry with you. I can be mean when I want. You will never see it coming."

Looking at Jyn, the idea of revenge seems a strong possibility. He runs across the yard, and swings open the carriage door. His body is barely on the seat when the door slams shut behind him, and the carriage is off at top speed. Bouncing around the carriage's interior makes putting on his socks and shoes challenging.

***

When the carriage arrives at Matron Family Services' front door, he runs up the stairs and plows into a staff member waiting for him.

"Follow me. Matron Qyn is waiting for you," she says.

He and the staff member quickened their steps. Grabbing the door handle, he realizes his heart is beating in his ears, and his breaths are coming fast and hard. A thought comes to his mind: A deep breath to calm my nerves before opening the door.

With a concerned face, Iuot looks up from the papers he and Qyn are discussing. Then, his focus returns to the matter at hand. Sitting down in the chair nearest to the door, he is confused. They speak in the ancestral tongue, and he has no idea what they are saying.

Finally, Qyn acknowledges his presence. "Iuot has found a way for you to have a name. We worked all afternoon yesterday. Iuot and I contacted many people to get their opinions. Almost the entire homestead community has taken on your cause. They found a precedent in *The No Fir*. Iuot has agreed. By the end of the day, you will have a name, a new name."

"What do you mean by a new name?" he asks.

Qyn says, handing him a document, "I am getting ahead of myself. I contacted some resources in River Bend. Mara followed through on her threat. Jotre Jotu Mara (Aeat Ueqi Atau) does not exist in her family tree.

Mara & Jotu Family Tree (Amended)
Parents:
Mara Ana Hener (Atau Ionu Aeqi)
Born: 17th Day, 10th Month, 2089
Jotu Joun Ruth (Ueqi Ueqa Udon)
Born: 6th Day, 3rd Month, 2063
Deceased: 12th Day, 8th Month, 2135
Children:
Deba Mara Jotu (Aata Atau Ueqi)
Born: 1st Day, 2nd Month, 2118
Deceased: 1st Day, 2nd Month, 2118
Isac Jotu Mara (Eqat Ueqi Atau)
Born: 14th Day, 11th Month, 2124

Your brother, Isac, is now her only son. The banks have given Mara access to any assets you had." The reality of his situation hits him. His head drops. Iuot stands up and moves around the table. Bending down next to his ear, Iuot said, "Eiu."

He asks, "Eiu? What is that?"

"Your new name," Qyn informs him.

"Eiu," Iuot repeats.

Qyn explains, "This is the solution to your problem. According to *The No Fir*, you are adoptable. There is no age restriction. Iuot wants to adopt you as his second son if you are willing. Thus, the new name. All homestead sons' names start with a vowel that indicates their birth order in the family. You will be his second son, so your name starts with E. To indicate your adoption and not birth into Iuot's family, your name will end in the first two letters of the same gender parent. In your case, the letters are "iu". Making your name Eiu."

The young man before Iuot and Qyn looks lost in all the information. Iuot stands up and says something to Qyn. She nods. Iuot turns and leaves.

***

Qyn travels to the beverage sideboard in the corner of the room. She drops ice cubes into two short crystal glasses. Reaching under the table runner, a tall, clear crystal bottle with a dark liquid inside appears. After pouring two fingers width of the liquid over the ice cubes in each glass, Qyn returns the stopper to the bottle and the bottle back to its hiding place. On her way back to her chair, Qyn places one of the glasses before him. He takes the glass, swallowing all of its contents without thinking.

"What is that?" he asks, snapping back from wherever he had been.

Qyn says, "I call it a reality check. But if you want me to be specific, it is high-grade hooch. My sister, Byn, makes it on the homestead. We keep it around here for emergencies. You looked like there was an emergency or about to be."

Qyn continues, "Let's start from the beginning again. As of the close of business last night, you no longer exist as a member of Mara's family. It is worse than that; you no longer exist as far as society is concerned. By erasing your name from her family tree, Mara erased your existence. Without your name, you can't conduct any business. In a society built on business, you never were. The fact that you have a physical body and are a breathing person doesn't matter. This morning, your brother Isac is Mara's only living child."

"That is all it takes to end a life," he says.

"Unfortunately, yes. But you have a chance for a new life." Qyn responds. "After Adiu and her parents became aware of Mara's actions, their only concern was for you. Even though

Equo had to go home to care for their homestead, Iuot stayed at Adiu's apartment. Iuot and I sent telegrams to all the orthodox homesteading families, seeking their advice and guidance. Adiu met with a lawyer who deals in family law. The lawyer looked into ways to refute these actions. Modern law supports Mara's decision on the matter. Waiting for responses from the community took up most of the afternoon. Every family prayed for guidance. Then, they referred to passages in *The No Fir*. By exchanging telegrams, the community expressed its opinions and presented any questions. Both the telegraph company and Fir On had a busy afternoon. The three of us were preparing to eat the Evening Meal when the community presented the idea of adoption. Adiu and the lawyer reviewed the legality of such an adoption. He gave her a list of places and people to see so that Adiu could gather all the necessary documentation. After her return this morning, Iuot sent Adiu home to rest. She looked exhausted. I sent a staff member with Adiu, just in case. Iuot and I prayed for guidance. He is excited about the possibility. Iuot contacted Equo at their homestead last evening. According to their partnership contract, she has the final say in such matters. Equo said she needed to pray as well. When she returned with her answer, there was a list of possible issues. Equo also said that if the community felt these were not a problem or could be handled according to *The No Fir*, she would consider her final answer. Iuot and I returned to the community this morning with Equo's concerns. They stated that those problems didn't affect your adoption. Equo gave her blessing."

Qyn asks, "As your representative, I need to review the documents with you and give my consent. Do you have any questions?"

"Why would Iuot do this for me? Equo and he barely know me. How will this affect Adiu? What about our contract?" he asks.

Qyn says, "This is an unusual situation. The community and the lawyer believe this should be fine with a partnership in the future because you aren't blood-related, and you haven't lived together. The only catch is that Adiu must move to her homestead so that you may move in with the family. She has agreed to this."

"Qyn, do you still think I am Adiu's best option?" he asks.

She responds, "Let's pray to Fir On for guidance. The correct answer will come."

Qyn holds Eiu's hands as they pray together. When they finish praying, he has his answer. His name is Eiu, and he is Iuot's second son, a homesteader.

Eiu and Qyn review the adoption paperwork. He meets the requirements in the government's eyes as an orphan:

✓Law enforcement has no record of anyone looking for a missing person fitting his description.

✓He is not a person in the governmental records.

✓He does not have a legal name.

✓Being adopted by a homesteader makes the legal process minimal. Homesteaders don't hold standing in society or use any of society's services.

✓Homesteaders' only requirement is to list all members for the census rolls.

The next document is Eiu's birth certificate. Qyn makes a few calls concerning the date of birth. The year must reflect his age, but she can choose the month and day as his legal representative.

Qyn says, "You are old enough to choose yourself. When would you like to celebrate your birth?"

Eiu looks at his birth certificate. Iuot signed it as his father and dated it today. The place where his mother would sign is blank.

"Will Equo not be my mother?" he asks.

Qyn sits back and gathers her thoughts. "Equo cannot be your legal mother. In the orthodox homesteader community, there are two groups of children based on their gender and birth order. First-born children, no matter their gender, belong to their

mother. Their names start with an A. The following letter signi-
fies the mother's place in the birth order, and the last two letters
are the first two letters of the father's name. If Equo becomes
your legal mother, you and Adiu are siblings. Siblings can't marry
each other, even if one of them is adopted. Equo will need to
give her written permission for Iuot to adopt you. He is taking
that form back to their homestead for her signature. Even without paperwork, you will be a son to Equo in her mind and heart.
So don't be surprised when she bosses you around. That is just
Equo saying you are part of the family."

After a moment, Eiu says, "Today is my birth date. I have a
new life today. I want to celebrate it each year." Qyn smiles ap-
provingly. With that settled, the remainder of the paperwork goes
smoothly. Each knock on the meeting room door brings new
documents with instructions on where to sign and initial.

Record of Birth

Eiu Iuot Udon
Adopted, age 39 years
11th Day, 6th Month, 2120
Parent: Iuot Otau Udon

Eiu tells Qyn, "I wish to thank Adiu for all she has done for
me. More than ever, I desire to be Adiu's partner. My new name
is also growing on me. I like being a son to a man with a high

moral standing. It is also easy to say, E I U."

When Eiu and Qyn are finished for the day, Qyn says, "Iuot says you should go to the homestead with him. He will be here in a little while. Adiu has moved her things from their homestead and will gather the last items in her apartment tonight. She will be heading to her homestead in the morning."

After taking a deep breath, Qyn says, "You and I must discuss a matter in the morning. So come back here after Morning Meal and Wisdom Studies."

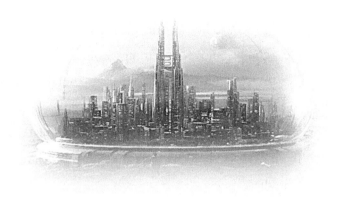

Chapter 12

Eiu's Debt

Twentieth Day, Fourth Month, 2159

After the evening meal, Equo pulls Eiu from the table. She hands him a drying cloth and, dipping her hand into the hot rinse water, shows him a fork.

Then Equo says, "Pron," with a long o sound. Eiu doesn't know what she is doing. Equo repeats the word slowly two more times. Waving the fork in front of his face, almost hitting him in the nose and eyes, Equo says the word for a fourth time. Eiu can see she is becoming frustrated with him.

Eiu wonders: What does she want from me? Finally, Equo has had enough. She grabs the lower part of his jaw inside his mouth with the three middle fingers of her other hand. Equo looks down his throat. Removing her hand, Equo smacks him on the left side of his face.

"Pron?" Eiu guesses. Equo nods enthusiastically. She hands him the fork to dry. Removing each piece of dinnerware from the water, Equo pronounces its name in their ancestral tongue and waits for Eiu to repeat it.

Equo moves closer, looks straight at him, and repeats the word when Eiu makes a mistake. As he struggles, her head shakes, and she seems dismayed. When Eiu gets the answer correct, Equo's countenance lights up. This discussion continues until everything is dried and put away.

Adiu's younger brother, Ateq, now Eiu's older brother, takes him to a room at the back of the house. "This is your room. Mama found some of Papa's and my clothes, which she thinks will fit you. She has already looked through her pattern stash. When Mama takes you to see the Matron, she will go to the mercantile for zippers and buttons. You will have new clothes in no time."

"She will make them for me?" Eiu asks.

Ateq responds, "Of course. Mama would die before allowing store-bought clothes in her house. She spins the sheep's wool and flax to make yarn and thread. Typically, she weaves cloth on her loom, but this is the birthing season, and all the mothers and newborns need her attention. Other homestead families have dropped off or sent fabric. Once they were informed you were joining our family, everyone in the community pitched in to assist with your transition."

Eiu is amazed by the generosity. "How do you feel about this?" he asks.

Ateq says, "Relieved. With Adiu taking her share of the homestead, there will be plenty of work to build up inventory and replace the hardware and machinery. I will miss her work here, though."

After the Morning Meal, Ateq spends the Wisdom Studies time helping Eiu learn how to read the ancestral tongue in *The No Fir.*

When Equo calls him from the carriage, Eiu hurries across the yard. He sits in the driver's seat with her, a sign of his growing confidence. Equo points out different things and tells him their ancestral tongue names as they travel. She looks cross at Eiu's mispronounced attempts, but he keeps trying. Other times, Equo laughs or lightly smacks his shoulder.

***

At about four, Equo and Eiu arrive at the Matron Family Services' office. Not for the first time, Eiu wonders what important matter Qyn had looking so grim yesterday. A staff member knocks softly on Qyn's office door.

"Come in. What do you need?"

Eiu pokes his head around the partially open door. "You said we must meet today."

Qyn says, "Oh, it is you. Give me a little time to finish this. It must go in the midday mail. Harriet, are you lurking outside my door? If so, take Eiu down to my meeting room. See if he wants something to drink while he is waiting. The baked goods look exceptionally tasty today."

Harriet and Eiu walk down the hallway and into the now-familiar meeting room. Eiu chooses coffee with a dash of cold cream and a pastry. Harriet refills his cup when Qyn enters the room, carrying a folder.

Qyn says, "Do you remember when I told you there would be consequences if you broke the contract? When Mara revoked your name, you lost the promised assets in the partnership contract. You cannot replace their value at this time. Although it is not your fault, it is your responsibility. You broke the contract and have a debt you must repay."

"What do you mean I have a debt? To Whom? How much?" Eui asks.

Qyn says, "You have a debt to Adiu," showing him a document.

> ### *Penalty for Breaking Partnership Contract*
>
> *Eiu Iuot Otau is indebted to Adiu Equo Iuot for 6,151 colonial units committed as dowry in the form of goods and monetary capital in a partnership contract.*
>
> *Matron Family Services*

"Adiu knows I cannot pay that. What game is she playing?" Eiu jumps up from his chair and begins pacing the room.

Qyn says, "Please sit back down. Adiu is not playing a game. Based on the contract you both signed, she is within her rights to collect damages for breaking the agreement."

"What happens if I refuse to pay this?" Eiu asks.

Qyn says, "Your father will have to pay the bill."

"Good luck with that. My father has been dead for decades," Eiu replies.

Qyn says, "I asked you the first time. Now, I am telling you to sit down before I call to have you arrested for failure to meet your obligations."

Footsteps are running down the hallway toward the meeting room. Myn and her staff member throw open the door, looking for the culprit, causing Qyn to raise her voice.

Qyn says, "Everything is fine. Eiu momentarily forgot himself. See, he is going to sit in the chair." Eiu shivers as he feels the bolts of lightning radiating from Myn's and her staff member's eyes. He sits down in the chair and remains silent.

Qyn continues, "I can handle things from here. I need only remind Eiu that less than one day ago, he was without a name or a family and did not exist in the eyes of society."

The pieces fall into place for Eiu. I do have a father. Iuot adopted me, so I have my name and a place in the homesteading community. How could I forget so quickly? Am I that ungrateful? Then, Eiu's mind goes to Adiu. Adiu could have walked away. But she and her family didn't do that. They embraced me in my time of need. The whole community came together to support and care for me. Eiu hangs his head in shame. Tears sting his eyes.

Qyn pulls a handkerchief from her sleeve and hands it to him. "Enough of that. Adiu did you a favor. The amount on that paper is just what you promised to bring to the partnership. In this folder, I have the expenses she has incurred." Qyn hands the folder over to Eiu. The top sheet details the cost of Mara's round-trip ticket and his one-way ticket, as well as the food, drink, and services provided by the train attendant.

"I thought these transportation costs were part of your services," says Eiu.

Planet 13 Interurban Train Service

One-Way First Class Ticket - Mr. Jotre Jotu Mara
(Includes 13% Carriage Attendant Gratuity): **Nu 6,194.69**

Round Trip First Class Ticket - Mrs. Mara Ana Hener
(Includes 13% Carriage Attendant Gratuity): **Nu 12,389.38**

Premium Tea Service *(Includes 13% Gratuity):* **Nu 1,019.28**

Gentlemen's Dressing Room Services
        (Includes 13% Gratuity):   **Nu 1,548.67**
Ladies' Dressing Room Services
        (Includes 13% Gratuity):   **Nu 3,097.35**

Total Amount Paid: **Nu 24,249.37**

*** All payments must be in Nu currency units ***

Qyn says, "Keep reading." The next invoice is for the hotel where Mara stayed, including the services of a full-time attendant, meals and drinks, and transportation.

Ephrata Premier Hotel

Penthouse Suite *(1,300 colonial units per night, four nights):*
$$Nu\ 5,200.00$$

Hotel Room Tax: *(13% fee per night, plus13% processing fee):*
$$Nu\ 1,469.00$$

Meals *(Including 13% gratuity):*   Nu 763.88
Daily Maid Service *(Including 13% gratuity):*   Nu 190.97
Laundry Service: *(Including 13% gratituity):*   Nu 84.50
Personal Driver *(Seven trips, including 13% gratuity):*
$$Nu\ 485.58$$

Total Amount Due: Nu 8,869.9
*** All payments must be in Nu currency units ***

Total Amount Paid: Nu 8,869.93

"How did Mother run up such a bill? Why didn't she pay it before she left?" he asks. Eiu realizes the answer at once. For the same reason, I didn't inquire about train journey costs. My mother and I assumed Qyn took care of it—it was just part of the service!

Sonnon Shuttle Stop Apartments

Apartment Lease Fee: *1,300 Nu currency units/month*
    (Thirteen Months):   Nu *16,900.00*
Deposit *(13% non-refundable fee):*   Nu *2,197.00*
Utility Deposit *(13% non-refundable fee):*   Nu *1,098.50*

Total Amount Due: Nu 20,195.50
    *** All payments must be in Nu currency units***

Total Amount Paid: Nu 20,195.50

The fifth and final sheet is an invoice for Qyn's services and those of her staff. It included all the payments Adiu had made so far.

Matron Contracted Partnership Services
Adiu Equo Iuot

Deposit *(Non-Returnable Fee):*   1,577.23 colonial units
**Total Payments Made:*   18,926.81 colonial units

Total Amount Paid: 20,504.04 colonial units

With a hard swallow, Eiu asks, "How much of this am I responsible for?"

Using a clean piece of paper on the table, Qyn copies the totals of each invoice and adds up the dowry, train journey, and hotel payments:

Monetary Value of Dowry: Nu 6,151.60
Train Journey: Nu 24,249.37
Hotel: Nu 8,869.93
Apartment: Nu 20,195.50
Exchange Rate (13%): Nu 7,730.63
*   Total Payments Made: Nu 6,7197.03*
Partnership Services: Cu 20,504.04

Total: Cu 87,701.07

Passing it back to him, Qyn says, "*The No Fir* requires Adiu to take some compensation for her losses. She only chose to take what you have promised in the contract."

"What can I do to make this right? I do not have a job," Eiu replies.

"Oh, but you do. As Iuot's second son, you receive one-eighth of the annual profits from the homestead. After telegramming Equo this morning, I calculated that you can pay the amount Adiu asks for in one year. You must work on the homestead for six and one-half years to pay the expenses for which you are responsible. To pay for Adiu's expenses, you must work for an additional six and one-half years. Because of the broken contract and incurred debt, you can't sign a new partnership contract until you have paid the debt," Qyn says.

His face falls again. "Have you talked to Adiu?"

"I have. Adiu needs to know your intentions before making any decisions."

"What do you think I should do?" Eiu asks Qyn.

Qyn replies, "I can't tell you that. I will say this. You told me you were proud to be the son of a man with high moral standards. Are you the son who will make a man of high moral standards proud?"

"Will you pray with me for Fir On's guidance?" asks Eiu.

Qyn says, "Of course, Eiu." Eiu grabs her hands and holds them so their edges touch his forehead.

"Fir On, I have been given so much by people in the last few days. I know I have not lived my life to the best of my ability. I know that nothing I have done in my life comes close to me deserving any of this. I also know I am not worthy of the blessings you have given me. I can't guarantee not to make mistakes, but I will try to give my best. Please watch over my old family. They have not lived easy lives. If you can bless them with your love, I would be grateful. As for my new family, please delay the time before they realize what a task they have taken on with me. Especially watch over Adiu. She has taken on monumental burdens, financially and personally. Please allow me to prove that her belief in me is well-spent. Thank you again." This time, Qyn takes her handkerchief out of her other sleeve. She tries to regain her composure, but her body will not cooperate. Eiu comes around the table and holds Qyn in his arms.

"I have come to a decision, Qyn. Paying my share of the debt will take six and a half years. I will work on the homestead for as long as it takes to pay all the debt Adiu has taken on," Eiu says. Qyn begins crying and sobbing in earnest. She tries but can't speak.

"Knock that off already. You are going to make me cry. Then I may realize what I have committed myself to and change my mind," Eiu says with a smile.

***

Equo waits outside next to the horses when Eiu exits the building. He runs over and puts his arms around her. With Equo firmly held in his arms, Eiu picks her off the ground and swings both of them in circles. Equo says something in the ancestors' tongue he doesn't understand. Almost dizzy, Eiu places her down on the ground. Equo grabs the bridle to steady herself.

When she finds her footing again, Equo takes the whip from its place on the driver's seat. She sends the whip cracking off his bottom. Eiu races around the back of the wagon and into the opposite side of the driver's seat. He lowers his hand to help Equo up. She smacks it away.

Once seated in the driver's position, Equo looks upward, muttering something Eiu doesn't understand. Without saying another word, she hands him the reins. Traveling home, Equo uses her arms and legs to direct Eiu's movements. Once, she even threatens him with the whip.

Chapter 13

Mara's Early Years

2094 to 2118

Mara arrives at the Grand Haven Train Station over an hour late. Katerina is waiting on the platform. The other ladies in her carriage take their time to gather themselves and their things. Sitting nearest the hallway, Mara has two choices: wait and exit through the cabin doors or risk waiting in the hallway and exit through the vestibule door. Mara sits in her seat. A cool breeze enters the room. Her luggage enters Mara's view on its way to the luggage pick-up area.

Katerina hugs Mara, "How was your journey?"

"Third class is a cattle car. Others are coming and going at all hours. Bumping and asking to move past kept me awake. The general public doesn't know they smell. It is not good. I sprayed perfume into my handkerchief, placing it near my nose," Mara says.

Katerina says, "Let's get your bags and go home. Do you have your luggage tickets?"

Mara hands them to the luggage ticket agent.

Katerina lets out a low whistle. "Is this everything?"

Mara's face looks cross; then she sees Katerina's smile. "Hopefully not. What will I do at the stores? Let's find a porter and a taxi," Mara says.

Four metal trunks create an obstacle course in the sitting room. The exhausted ladies flop into a pair of reclining chairs.

Katerina asks, "Do you want to talk?"

"Not yet," Mara says. The digital clock signals it is time for the Midday Meal.

Katerina says, "Let me see what I have available. How about a bath or shower until it is ready?"

"Yes! The scrub brush and I have a date. See you once other people's dirt and smells are washed down the drain," says Mara.

Katerina notices Mara acting more like herself during the meal. She lugs one of the giant trunks into the second bedroom.

"Do you have extra hangers?" Mara asks.

A bell rings in another room. Katerina says, "The mail has arrived. Do you want to go along? We can take the luggage dolly back to the lobby."

"Yes. I should have some mail. I transferred my address here before I left the hotel. I am looking for some important documents," Mara replies.

While they wait in line, the discussion turns to matters to handle within the next few days. Mara recalls: Katerina moved here after her second husband passed away. It is rent-controlled and includes utilities. The other renters have jobs or activities outside the building. So she is alone during the day. When I called, Katerina was happy to have me move in. I offered to pay the second resident charge and one-half of the rent. This will reduce both of our expenses.

Mara receives several standard envelopes and a sizable padded package. On their return trip, Katerina introduces her to Natala and her daughter, Gwyndolyn.

"Gwyndolyn will be leaving for Secondary School in the autumn. She has received a scholarship and will be a nurse after graduation. My sons work in marketing, finance, and sales. Edward, my husband, travels nine months a year. He is a personal lawyer for a professional athlete," says Natala. Neither Katerina nor Mara knows who he represents.

***

Taking glasses of iced tea into the sitting room, Mara asked, "Do you have a letter opener?" She slices through the top edge of the padded package. "I think I am ready to discuss something with you. Please don't judge me too harshly."

"How long have we been friends? I will do my best to understand," Katerina replies.

Mara says, "You are so kind. How could Jotre mistreat you so?"

"In looking back, Jotre was correct. I was not ready for a relationship so quickly after my divorce," says Katerina.

Mara says, "I have done something drastic. I want you to look through these documents." She heads to her bedroom for a pen while handing the package to Katerina.

Upon her return to the sitting room, Mara picks up her iced tea and remaining envelopes and goes to the kitchen. Listening to sounds from the sitting room, Mara looks at her invoices and bank statements. She makes notes. Picking up the telephone, Mara connects with her previous residence. The front desk clerk gives her a list of outstanding individual expenses and the total due. Putting these on her credit account finalizes her last attachment to Jotre. Mara heads into her bedroom. Lying down on the bed, her body shakes as Mara cries for her lost son.

Katerina leaves Mara to sleep through the Evening Meal. She thinks about the documents she read. Katerina wonders why Mara would do this. She loves Jotre. This explains why she needed to move away from her family. How is he? Should I contact Isac? How do I handle this?

3

***

During the Morning Meal, Katerina brooches the subject, "Are you ready to talk?"

"Can we wait until after we finish?" Mara asks.

Katerina says, "Whenever you are ready."

With dishes done and coffee in hand, they head into the sitting room. "I don't know where to start," Mara says.

Katerina replies, "Starting at the beginning works best for me."

"I don't know how much you know about my childhood," begins Mara.

Katerina says, "You haven't discussed much about the time before Jotu and you were married."

"My parents couldn't afford Secondary School. I became a live-in housekeeper for Jotu and his wife Evi at thirteen. They lived in a penthouse condominium in the upper society area of Lebanon. I attended classes during the day and cleaned each night. Albert, the butler, handled the rest of the household duties. They had social engagements most nights, leaving Albert and me alone to eat in the kitchen. He handled the meal if they were in for the evening, and I took a plate to my room. Those nights, I studied. In my early twenties, higher-end restaurants began catering, so Albert's meal duties centered on service. Evi created a housekeeping schedule based on their social engagements. I remained available until everyone went to bed if they had overnight guests. Albert worked even later and started earlier the next morning. I liked the summer and winter. Jotu and Evi traveled to their friends' second homes. I took additional classes in subjects I liked. The classes were smaller, with most students going home for vacation between semesters," Mara says. "When I was twenty-five, a parked truck lost its brakes and careened down a street. Coming back from the opera, Jotu and Evi's taxi was plowed into, sending it into parked cars until it stopped in the middle of an intersection. The most significant damage occurred on Evi's passenger door. Ambulances raced to the nearest hospital. Jotu and the driver required surgery, but Evi died on the way. Jotu returned home emotionally wounded and melancholy. Albert took over the household finances. Heat-up deli meals replaced the catered ones. Managers and colleagues made weekly phone calls and sent meals, but their friends only sent flowers. I read articles of interest to him," continues Mara.

"About a year later, I found Jotu and Albert reviewing the finances. Each day, Jotu tackled another part of his life. The three of us ate in the kitchen together. We discussed events in our lives. Soon, Albert was purchasing food from the local market to cook. After six months, Jotu returned to work. Arriving home one evening, Jotu asked, "Are you happy here?" I replied that the condominium was a beautiful and comfortable place. Jotu continued, "You are about to graduate. It has been brought to my attention that it may seem improper for you, as a single lady, to remain in my house afterward. I am your employer, and our contract is coming to an end. I want you to be presented to society. I will sponsor you. The debutante balls begin in three months," says Mara. "In a few days, dressmakers, cotillion instructors, shoemakers, and dance teachers rang our bell with their tools and materials. I was invited to participate in the first high society ball of the season. I practiced every spare moment and dreamed about it every night. More invitations came daily. Jotu and I sat in the kitchen, placing each event on the calendar," Mara continues. "Jotu and I began attending social engagements on the weekends. He explained theater presentations, museum exhibits, garden arrangements, and afternoon teas. Focus and intensity took over my studies. Jotu and Albert discussed the subjects I was studying and answered my questions. This was one of the happiest times of my life."

Mara hesitates, then says, "I hope my memories are not boring you."

Katerina says, "Quite to the contrary. I find it fascinating. Please go on."

"Then the ball season began. The houses were beautiful. The food was delicious. The gowns and suits were magnificent. The music was delightful. My dance card was filled every night. But the conversations were dull—the girls vied for marriage to the wealthiest families, and the boys were concerned with their toys and having fun. The gossip was all about inappropriate behavior. I sat near Jotu during the meals, listening to the adults. The ball season ended with several debutantes dating or engaged, but I was not one of them," Mara says.

Katerina asks, "How did you feel about that?"

"To be asked would have been nice, but I wasn't interested in any of the boys or being married to them. This situation bothered Jotu more than me. I enjoyed the social events held by the upper class. That was enough. In the summer, we were invited to escape the heat in the city at others' second homes or getaways on the weekends. The ladies played badminton and croquet in the afternoons. The men practiced shooting clay pigeons. Everyone dressed for dinner. The men retired to the billiard room with snifters of brandy afterward. The women played cards and listened to music on the record player in the lounge. These evenings went into the early morning," Mara replies.

Mara says, "During the week, Albert and I would attend the cinema. Government-approved movies became repetitious in their plots and endings. Those who follow the rules prosper, and those who don't are punished. The guy or girl may fall in love with someone from another class, but he or she will do the right thing, leaving behind their love to be abandoned by their family and society. Then autumn came. One night after dinner, Jotu said,

"You know I care for you." I replied, "I know. You have been very kind to me, and I care about you, too." Jotu said, "Mara Ana, I don't want you to leave, but if you stay, people will think bad about us both. I have been considering the options. I know it is not romantic, but the situation would be resolved if we were getting married." I said, "Jotu, I don't want to leave you either. I have grown quite fond of you. We enjoy our life together. Why should we change that? I would be honored to be your wife." The next afternoon, Jotu and I went to a jeweler's and picked out an engagement ring and two wedding bands. We attended the Cotillion season as an engaged couple. Jotu and I danced together like we had been doing it all our lives. I was welcome to sit with the married ladies and invited to afternoon teas and luncheons. I had a group of friends for the first time. The ladies and I discussed everything a married woman needs to know. I invited them to our house as well. Jotu and I hosted dinners. As soon as the season was over, Jotu and I were married in a simple service in the local chapel. Our friends were there in mass. We were so happy together."

Mara continues, "Less than six months later, we discovered I was pregnant. Jotu was shocked by the news. He was fifty-four years old. He and Evi did not have children. Jotu thought he could not have them, so we didn't use prevention. Jotu and I were elated by the news. Everything was going along well until my tenth month. I felt queasy in the evening, but neither Jotu nor I was concerned; this happened often during my pregnancy. Just before the Morning Meal, I had severe stomach cramps, and blood poured down my legs. Albert drove us to the nearest hospital. I was raced into surgery. Awaking in the recovery room, the doctor explained what had happened. The umbilical cord was twisted twice around our daughter's neck. She had starved. My body's instinct took over, trying to expel her. In doing so, my amniotic sack was torn, resulting in internal bleeding. They were able to remove her and the sac vaginally. They sewed up the leaks. She was dead." Mara hands Katerina two pieces of paper.

Record of Birth

Deba Mara Jotu (Aata Atau Ueqi)
Born - 1st Day, 2nd Month, 2118
Parents:
Mara Ana Hener (Atau Ionu Aeqi)
Jotu Joun Ruth (Ueqi Ueqa Udon)

Record of Death

Deba Mara Jotu (Aata Atau Ueqi)
Deceased at Birth - 1st Day, 2nd Month, 2118
Parents:
Mara Ana Hener (Atau Ionu Aeqi)
Jotu Joun Ruth (Ueqi Ueqa Udon)

Mara is visibly shaking, tears falling down her face. The Evening Meal bell rings. Mara excuses herself and heads to the bathroom. Katerina feels great sorrow for her friend. She thinks: We made the choice not to have children. For Mara to lose a child, especially a daughter, is a significant loss. Women lead the homesteader families. Firstborn daughters are considered a great blessing. Even without following the orthodox ways, Mara had to be devastated.

When the meal is ready, Katerina looks for Mara. She lies on top of the bed covers. Katerina brings a throw from the sitting room. She finishes the Evening Meal alone and heads to her bedroom.

Mara appears in the kitchen just before the Morning Meal the next day. Katerina places a plate of food in front of her. Mara pours herself a cup of coffee from the pot on the table.

Katerina asks, "How did you sleep?"

"Surprisingly well. I think I just needed to get things out of my system. It felt good to talk about it. At the time, Jotu was handling everything. I remained in the hospital for two weeks. Every time I closed my eyes, I saw our dead little daughter. The doctor gave orders for sedative injections so I could sleep. Some of the nightmares were so vivid I would scream and fight everyone who came near me. I woke up with restraints on my arms and legs several times. I was so ashamed of my behavior; it felt like I had lost control of my mind and body. Jotu would visit me after work each day. The nurses were so kind to me. They would take me for a shower after the Midday Meal and help me change into the dressing gowns Jotu brought. Some of the gowns were new and in beautiful dark colors: emerald, ruby, and purple. Their kindness only made me feel worse about my actions," Mara replies.

"When it was time to go home, Jotu told me that he had hired a caretaker to be with me when he was at work. Albert would take care of the apartment duties and bring meals. Jotu also told me that the doctor was sending home vials of the medication they had used in the hospital with needles so I would continue to heal and rest. I hated to have Jotu see me like this! What had Albert been told? The nightmares decreased over time, and my medication was changed to capsules," says Mara.

Chapter 14

Mara's Later Years

2118 to 2159

"Jotu and I returned to the activities we enjoyed with a new appreciation for our lives together. We traveled to foreign lands using super-speed trains for our vacations. When Jotu retired at sixty, we took a year-long trip worldwide. Jotu and I stayed in luxurious hotels and had great adventures. When we returned, I started feeling nauseous several times a day. Jotu thought it was due to all the travel. After seeing a doctor, I was surprised to learn I was pregnant again. I didn't know how Jotu would react. The doctor recommended bed rest and weekly checkups," Mara continues.

"When Albert and I returned home, I began pacing the floor with many thoughts cluttering my mind. Finally, Albert convinced me to sit down and have something to eat and drink. He sat with me until Jotu came home from a board meeting. I took a deep breath and blurted out the news. Although Jotu was surprised, he was also delighted. Jotu attended every weekly checkup and took me out for afternoon tea afterward. In retirement, Jotu and I made new friends through the different charity organizations we joined. They were caring and kind. The nausea continued until it was replaced with kicking. The kicking was strong, and the baby moved a lot. Jotu and I took these as signs that our child was healthy," says Mara.

"On my due date, I began to feel severe cramps. Jotu started to measure the time between my cramps. Then they just stopped. Albert made a doctor's appointment for the following day. The doctor laughed at us when we told him what happened and reminded us that these were practice contractions. After checking, he assured us that everything was fine. The practice contractions occurred several times a day for the next two weeks. Then, one night, at 1:00, I felt a contraction harder than the previous ones. At first, I did my breathing exercises, and we waited for them to stop. But they became stronger, and the time between them decreased over the next several hours. At 4:00, Jotu called our doctor's office and left a message. An hour later, his physician's assistant told us to go to the hospital. Jotre Jotu Mara was born less than forty-five minutes after we arrived at the hospital. He weighed ten pounds and twelve ounces. Jotre was twenty-two inches long and a head long, black hair. Breastfeeding him came naturally. Jotu and I were so happy." Mara says and hands Katerina a document:

Record of Birth

Jotre Jotu Mara (Aeat Ueqi Atau)
Born 20th Day, 8th Month, 2123
Parents:
Mara Ana Hener (Atau Ionu Aeqi)
Jotu Joun Ruth (Ueqi Ueqa Udon)

"We spent our days caring for Jotre. Jotu purchased a wedge so I could lie at an angle on the chaise lounge in our bedroom when breastfeeding. People stopped by, bringing meals and presents. Jotre allowed them to hold him without even a whimper. In three weeks, he slept from 10:00 until 0:00 and, after a feeding and a diaper change, from 1:00 to 4:00 Jotu and I took turns carrying him in a sling on walks and trips to art galleries, museums, and gardens. We were closer than ever before," Mara says, smiling.

"It was not until after Jotre was six months old that I realized I had missed my monthly cycle. I could not remember when I last had it. I had been breastfeeding during this time, so I should not have been able to get pregnant. I talked to my doctor about missing my monthly cycle at my post-delivery checkup. He took some blood for testing and did a gynecological exam. I was pregnant again. Less than eleven months later, another healthy baby boy was born." Mara says, as she sorts through her pile of papers, and gives one to Katerina:

Record of Birth

Isac Jotu Mara (Eqat Ueqi Atau)
Born 14th Day, 11th Month, 2124
Parents:
Mara Ana Hener (Atau Ionu Aeqi)
Jotu Joun Ruth (Ueqi Ueqa Udon)

"After two successful births resulting in male heirs, Jotu and I decided we had been blessed enough with children. I spent two additional days in the hospital to recover from womb removal surgery," states Mara.

"As a family, we traveled with Albert and a nanny named Jeanette. The boys learned by experiencing educational in-person adventures. They were taking classes through the mail. Jotre and Isac took an intelligence test and scored in the upper ten percent. We didn't have a care in the world. Jotu took care of our finances, so I never had to worry about how much we spent," Mara recalls.

"Our family made new friends along the way. They invited us to stay with them or in their second homes. This continued until Jotu turned seventy years old. He had problems sleeping through the night, walking long distances, and was using the bathroom more frequently. Jotu and I decided it was time to go home. The boys would finish their primary education at a private school that friends recommended. This left Jotu, Albert, and I alone in the condominium. Isac came home for breaks, but Jotre stayed to take additional elective classes," says Mara.

"When Jotre was twelve and Isac was eleven, Jotu suffered a stroke. He remained in the hospital for more than a month. The doctors said Jotu had been having minor strokes for a while. I contacted the boys' secondary school, requesting Jotre and Isac come home. They arrived the day after another stroke took Jotu's life. We buried him in the family plot," says Mara, with tears in her eyes. Katerina receives Jotu's amended death certificate.

Record of Death (Amended)

Jotu Joun Ruth (Ueqi Ueqa Udon)
Deceased - 12th Day, 8th Month, 2135
Partner:
Mara Ana Hener (Atau Ionu Aeqi)
Children:
Deba Mara Jotu (Aata Atau Ueqi) - Deceased
Isac Jotu Mara (Eqat Ueqi Atau)

"I didn't want to be alone, so I asked Isac to stay with me. He could finish his studies in a school in the city. Jotre was in his next to last year, so he returned to Secondary School. Jotu's colleagues at work attended the funeral and graveside service. They sent meals and flowers for an entire year. Their wives invited me out for meals and social activities. I joined social service groups, donating my time and money to many causes. Isac and Albert took great care of me after I lost Jotu," Mara says.

"You remember the day several large banks filed for bankruptcy?" Mara asks.

Katerina replies, "Yes, my husband lost his job shortly afterward. We moved in with my parents. It took over ten years for the economy to return to normal."

"Our bank froze its customers' accounts. Jotu and I had developed a plan in case we lost access to our bank security box. We kept a quantity of liquid assets like currency, stocks, and bonds at home in case of an emergency. I opened our safe. There were over 100,000 colonial units in cash and the same amount in stocks and bonds. The condominium mortgage was paid off before Jotu retired. Our family could ride the situation out if we tightened our financial belts. We were fortunate," Mara says.

"When people could purchase housing again, the housing market boomed. Jotre convinced me to sell our condominium. It sold for over three times what Jotu paid for it. I had a significant nest egg. Enough to pay my expenses for the rest of my life if I lived frugally. Jotre found me the rent-controlled apartment I was living in before I moved in with you. For taking care of me so well, I promised Jotre I would set aside 250,000 colonial units as his firstborn legacy," Mara continues.

"But after ten years of living with such modesty, I was ready to splurge. I sold my fancy attire at a consignment shop. I planned only to spend the money I made from the shop, but the new stores held so many treasures I just had to have. I redecorated my entire apartment, one room at a time. There was always something else that would complete the look. I treated myself to new seasonal clothing and shoes. I decided to have my meals delivered from local restaurants. Their price was much less than our family had paid for meals at the condominium. I hired a laundry service. A service came into my apartment every two weeks to clean. I traveled to a nearby cafe each morning for coffee and pastry. Before I realized it, I barely had enough money to pay my rent and utilities. My money was gone, and I also spent Jotre's inheritance. I went to Isac because I was too ashamed to tell Jotre. For the last decade, Isac has been paying my bills," says Mara.

"When I met Adiu Equo Iuot, I realized she was the perfect partner for Jotre. Although the dowry amount is not included in the partnership contract, I assumed Jotre listed the 250,000 colonial units I promised him. I won't let a homesteader know Jotre has nothing financially to offer. A digger looking down on me and my family is unacceptable. Then, I discovered Adiu and Jotre will live on a homestead she owns. That was the last straw! I haven't worked so long and hard to move off the homestead only to have Jotre return there. I would lose Jotre to her," continues Mara.

"After thinking about the situation overnight, I knew I had to take drastic action. I called a lawyer friend to weigh my options. If I renounced Jotre as my son, I would force him to come to me if he wanted his life back. I will make conditions for Jotre's return to the family based on his breaking the partnership contract and begging my forgiveness for pursuing such a ludicrous idea. I knew I had lost him for good when he didn't contact me within twenty-six hours. My plan hasn't worked the way I expected. How does he think he will survive without a name?" Mara said.

Katerina says, "I don't know. Did he send a telegram or make a call? I can contact the front desk to ask if any visitors or messages have arrived. This must be unpleasant for you. Is there anything else I can do?"

"No. I have contacted an auctioneer about having an estate sale for his house and personal things. His business and tools will also be sold. This will give me enough money to pay my expenses here and have a little spending money. Isac has agreed to supplement that amount each month. He has always been there when I need him and understands me better than anyone," Mara replies.

Katerina remains silent.

"I did what I had to do. I had no choice. He is intelligent and resourceful. In a few more days, I will hear from him. When he does, I will explain everything to him. He will understand. Isac understood when I told him," says Mara.

Katerina sees the anguish on her friend's face. "I know you meant him no harm. It is about time for the Midday meal. Let's go out—my treat. Maybe we do a little shopping on our way back."

Chapter 15

Adiu's Next Three Months
Twentieth Day, Fourth Month until
Nineteenth Day, Seventh Month 2159

The day after Papa sends Adiu back to her apartment to rest, she begins packing up her smaller items. Ateq arrives just before the Midday meal, and Adiu shows him Ephrata. He is fascinated by all the things in the store windows.

Adiu takes Ateq to her favorite restaurant. It is on the top floor of a department store. She tells Ateq to push the number four elevator button. He falls backward when the elevator begins to move. Ateq holds the rail tightly until the ride is done. When the elevator doors open wide, so do his eyes. There are round wooden tables with chairs everywhere in the large room. A young woman leads them to a table with two wooden chairs. She returns shortly with two glasses of iced water, a teapot, and two small cups. There are placemats, silverware, napkins, and chopsticks on the table. Ateq picks up the chopsticks and asks, "What are these?"

"They are chopsticks. Some people eat and cook with them. I learned how to use them." Adiu shows Ateq, and he tries to mimic her actions. The chopsticks will not cooperate. Both of them laugh.

Just then, a woman pushes a cart up to their table and lifts the lid of a small, round metal container. Inside are dough balls covered in sesame seeds. Adiu puts up one finger. The woman removes the sesame balls from their container and places them on a small plate. She hands it to Adiu. Placing the plate on the table between them, Adiu explains, "These are red bean paste and sesame seed steamed buns. The red bean paste is sweet. Try one."

Adiu picks one of the balls up with her fingers and pops it into her mouth. Ateq does the same. He smiles, "I like that."

A series of women approach their table with carts laden with similar metal containers, each containing a different type of food. Adiu indicates if she wants any or how many. Ateq is happy when Adiu doesn't order the chicken feet. Adiu uses her chopsticks to pick up individual portions and place them on the larger plates in front of them. She describes each to Ateq.

Ateq attempts to use the chopsticks and then grabs his fork. When the plates are empty, Adiu places them on top of each other near the table's edge. They talk about the tasks at hand and make plans.

"Mama and Papa went over to your homestead and erected a yurt for you to live in while all the work is happening. I will bring over the stuff from our place once you are ready. Have you contacted anyone about your house and utilities?" Ateq says.

Adiu replies, "Yes. Oasi's sons are building the house. I chose to use bamboo for the pillars and walls. Straw and dirt adobe will be plastered on top. Ieoc will be laying paving stones with grout for the floors. I have chosen not to have any indoor plumbing work. The underground stream is close enough to the house and livestock barn. A hydroelectric system will be connected to the stream."

Adiu continues, "The house will have two bed chambers, a kitchen/dining area, and a sitting room. The bed chambers will be the only rooms with full-height interior walls. Next to the second bed chamber will be a bathroom with a door leading outside. The root cellar will be under the kitchen/dining area, with a ladder in the pantry. The stream will pass under a water mill to provide additional electricity and mill grain."

Adiu says, "The utility inspector told me the fan size I need to circulate the air. I ordered it this morning. Oasi's sons will pick it up at the train station. That should keep me busy for now."

"Have you thought about Eiu?" asks Ateq.

Adiu's face saddens, and she answers, "Constantly. I struggle all the time with not seeing or talking to him. But Mama said we must avoid contact until Eiu pays the dowry. Then she will think about it."

Ateq knows better than to suggest he slip a message to Eiu. Adiu and Mama would be angry.

Adiu asks, "Have you had enough to eat?"

"More than enough. We should probably get to work," replies Ateq.

Adiu signals the woman who seated them. She counts the plates and hands Adiu the bill. She looks at the bill and hands the woman several Nu unit notes. Adiu says, "Please keep the change for the servers."

Back at Adiu's apartment, they begin loading the oversized furniture into the wagon. The smaller pieces and the boxes are loaded next. Finally, a tarp covering the wagon and its contents is tied down. Adiu goes to the apartment manager's office to do the final paperwork.

Ateq takes the reins, with Adiu beside him in the driver's seat. Their trip will take two days. Adiu and Ateq will spend a night with relatives and then continue.

***

When Adiu and Ateq arrive at their cousin's homestead, it is very late, and they are tired. A warm plate of food and a glass of milk greet them as they sit at the table. Hunger wins the battle against sleep. Adiu and Ateq devour the delicious food and drink several glasses of milk each. Ateq will sleep in the boys' room and Adiu in the girls' room. A cot with blankets and pillows is placed on the floor. Both sleep soundly until the Morning meal bell rings.

After the Morning meal and Wisdom studies, Adiu and Ateq say farewell and board the wagon. A basket of food sits on the floorboards between them.

Ateq is surprised when he is later directed to leave the underground dirt road and travel to a town under a dome. Traveling through the town, several people waved to Adiu. She waves back and has Ateq stop in front of a mail delivery office. He follows Adiu inside.

Waiting their turn, Adiu converses with a young girl with three little children. She introduces Naomi to Ateq. Adiu places an order for eggs, milk, and vegetables. Naomi's husband, Abel, will deliver the groceries on his route the next day. The agent greets Adiu by name and asks how her trip was. His name is Jakob. Ateq is introduced.

At the wagon, Ateq asks, "How do you know so many people?"

"This town is not part of the city. These people were sent here because they believe a deity with three parts rules the universe. The community purchased the land and had a dome built over it. They grow their food, make their clothing, and live a simple life. When I purchased my land from the railroad company, I asked who I could employ to dig my access road. Local businesses were suggested. This town is very good to me. The road maintenance company dug my access and put cement drainage pipes under the stream. They did all the work for only fifteen percent above cost and labor. Wait until you see the work they did on my driveway," Adiu says.

Adiu directs Ateq to the left. "See that mountain in front of us. I own a two-mile by two-mile section of it. The railroad company agreed to the purchase if I would allow them to use my access road to load and unload. The mountain above ground is considered unusable for building, so they were happy to sell it to me at a discounted price."

Upon arriving at the mountain's base, Ateq's mouth falls open. Beyond the railroad tracks, twelve-foot-high cement arches line the access road entrance. These continue for more than an eighth of a mile.

Still in shock, Ateq can't believe the scene before him. A vast cavern opens up with a considerable stream flowing down the middle. Adiu's yurt is situated on the right side of the entrance in the corner. The cavern walls are over thirteen feet tall. Ateq stops the wagon in front of the yurt, and they unload its contents.

When Adiu and Ateq finish, they return to the driver's seat. Adiu takes Ateq on a tour and explains her plans. "There is a large alcove at the back of the cavern. This will be the location of my house and barns. The stream flows through it."

Ateq can see the outstanding craftsmanship in the culvert construction. "Halfway between the cavern's entrance and back, a concrete bridge covers the stream. It is wide enough to drive farm equipment across. A pair of hand pumps sit across the stream from one another," continues Adiu.

"The other side of the cavern will be used for growing grains and vegetables. It will have food and equipment barns," Adiu says.

Ateq had been concerned about the quantity of equipment and animals Adiu would receive as her inheritance. He thought there would not be enough room, but this homestead is four times the size of their parents'.

Ateq thinks, Once I apply to be a partner, maybe I can convince Adiu to join them here. With this much room and my inheritance, my dowry could be persuasive when the time comes.

***

With the wagon tour over, Adiu and Ateq head back into Fertility to pick up the tables and benches for the workers. Ateq almost falls off his seat when Adiu tells him the town's name. They visit the butcher's after picking up a pair of submersible cooling boxes. They will act as refrigerators when placed in the stream.

The cavern has a year-round temperature near fifty degrees' universal temperature. The stream's temperature is colder. Once there are animals to slaughter, more cooling boxes will be added. Adiu and Ateq will pick up the meat after they have something to eat at the community restaurant.

Ateq orders scrapple and hash browns. He has yet to learn what they are, but Ateq likes the sound they make when he says them to the server.

"What did I order?" Ateq asks once the server has left their table.

Adiu grins widely. "You, my brother, ordered thick buckwheat and cornmeal porridge mixed with spices and ground organ meat, formed into a loaf, sliced and potatoes grated into shards, made into patties, and browned in butter. Scrapple gets its name because it is made with the scraps left over after butchering. You can eat it with honey."

Ateq takes in the information. "Is it good?"

"Yes, I like it for breakfast. I will be making some for myself," Adiu says. Their food arrives.

"What is that?" Ateq asks, looking at her plate.

"That is stuffed pig stomach. It is filled with sausage, cabbage, and potatoes and covered in brown gravy. We need to stop by the mercantile on the way back. I want to send back home honey and a dozen faschnachts," said Adiu.

Ateq asks, "What are faschnachts?

Planet Thirteen – Adiu & Jotre

"Faschnacht means the night before fasting. Deep-fried yeast-leaven flattened dough balls made with lard, sugar, fat, and butter. They are usually eaten the day before the forty days of restriction practiced by the townspeople. The mercantile owner's wife made some especially for you to take home. The banker's daughter, Ester, will pick you up after the Morning Meal and Wisdom studies tomorrow morning. She is traveling to her sister's house to care for her family until after their eighth child is born. Ester will drop you off at the shuttle stop. From there, you will connect with the main train back to Lewis. Mama will pick you up at the train station after doing her errands," says Adiu.

***

At 3:00 the next day, trucks and equipment roll into the homestead. Adiu is making coffee, and Ateq is loading pitchers of water, milk, and juice into a cooling box filled with stream water onto a table. Glasses, mugs, and teaspoons round out the provisions.

In a meeting with each crew's supervisor, Adiu reviews the schedule for the day and blueprints for the buildings. After the meeting, Adiu returns to her yurt. She and Ateq eat and complete their morning Wisdom studies. Just as they finish, Ester arrives.

As Ateq prepares to leave, he says, "Don't be too bossy, sister. Men don't like that."

"When have I ever been bossy?" Adiu asks.

Ateq says, winking at Adiu, "The better question is, when haven't you been bossy? Just be nicer to them than you are to me. Not every man is as easygoing as I am."

Ester opens her car's trunk. Ateq loads a box carrying a case of maple syrup and a bag of faschnachts. His satchel sits beside Ester's suitcase. Tears form as Adiu hugs her brother. Ateq will be at their parent's homestead before the Evening Meal.

Turning around to watch the work, Adiu hears the engine roar to life and tires crunch across the dirt. She walks to where Oasi's grandchildren are weaving the bamboo matting for the walls. Their fathers are marking the walls and rooms with chalk on the ground. Ieoc is with them discussing the placement of the paving stones. At one of the tables, Adiu will continue working on a design for the orchards, vegetable gardens, and grain fields.

Although she is pleased with the work, Adiu is relieved when the workers go home for lunch. She offered to make their lunch, but they refused.

The workers return just after Adiu finishes her Wisdom studies. Jona, one of the grandchildren, runs to Adiu with a book in his hand. He explains the book is called *Di Heilich Shrift*. It is a gift from Leah. This is the City Speak version. Adiu remembers, I was talking to his mother about the people in Fertility earlier. I told Leah I wanted to read the book they follow to understand their beliefs and culture better.

For the remainder of the day, Adiu unloads her trunks. She rearranges her furniture inside her yurt and puts things away in the wardrobe, on the tables, and in floor cabinets.

Outside the entrance to her yurt, a ring of large stones encircles the tripod legs of her cast iron cauldron. After everyone else leaves, Adiu lights the starter, waiting until the kindling catches fire. The larger sticks are placed on the pile, giving a warm glow. In a while, the water in the cauldron begins to bubble. Adiu carries a bucket of warm water into her sleeping area. A trip to the stream fills a second bucket with cold water. It has been too long since Adiu's last bath. Sitting in her nightgown and slippers near the fire, Adiu feels clean and content.

Chapter 16

After leaving Qyn's office in Ephrata, Mama and Eiu arrive at a homestead in chaos. Birthing season is in full swing, with pregnant sows, ewes, cows, nannies, and does in labor simultaneously. Ateq is taking Adiu and her things to her homestead and will not return for a few days.

Mama sends Eiu to find Papa. Papa is in the cattle barn, and his right arm is inside a cow. Eiu wonders, what is Papa doing inside the cow? Why is he doing it? Will the cow and calf be healthy?

Eiu stands outside the birthing pen for a moment—Papa motions toward a clipboard, number tags, and tag gun sitting on a chair. Papa mimes the task he wants Eiu to do with his left hand while talking in the ancestral tongue. Eiu will write down the mother's tag number and type of animal in the chart. Next, he will tag the left ear of her babies. The final step is to record their tag numbers. Eiu is to start in the cattle barn. Papa will join him once the calf has been turned and delivered.

When Eiu hesitates, Papa shoos him away. Entering the next birthing pen, he records the cow's tag number and the first one at the end of the tagging gun. Sitting down next to the calf, Eiu gently grabs its left ear, places the end of the gun against it, and pulls the trigger. The calf moans and runs towards its mother. Papa nods his head in approval.

Eiu moves around the cattle barn, repeating this process. In one pen, he discovers twins. How often are there multiple births? Eiu wonders. These and many other questions swirl inside his mind.

After recording the last calf, Eiu returns to Papa. Sitting with the cow, holding its calf in his arms, his hand is stroking the cow's side. Papa's eyes are closed, and he is silently praying. The calf is not moving. It takes Eiu a moment to realize the calf is dead. He also closes his eyes, praying to Fir On on behalf of the calf and its mother. Papa takes the calf from the birthing pen and wraps it in a sheet. Eiu follows him as Papa carries the body to Mama in another barn. She takes it from him. Papa motions Eiu to follow him.

At the pen containing the twin calves, Papa picks up one, carrying it in his arms. Returning to the cow without a calf, he lays the new calf next to the cow's teats. Papa pulls a teat, squirting milk into its mouth. The calf latches on, nursing. Eiu has tears running down his cheeks. Papa sees this and pats him gently on the shoulder. Eiu changes the birth record to reflect this new situation.

Papa takes the tagging gun, and Eiu keeps the clipboard. They travel from barn to barn, recording each birth.

In the sheep barn, each ewe has one lamb. All are healthy. Eiu knows pigs have multiple births, but he is amazed by how many piglets the two sows gave birth to—a total of twenty-six. Papa and Eiu find three that are dead, and two need to be bottle-fed. Both men pray for the piglets and their mothers. Papa wraps each dead piglet in a sheet and then hands them to Eiu. He takes them to Mama. Eiu turns quickly. He doesn't want to know what happens next to the dead animals.

In the goat barn, the four nannies have twenty kids. Only one of them will need additional attention. The number of dead and sickly kittens at the rabbit hutches is almost one-third. These kittens are removed. Papa quietly snaps the necks of ill ones. Seeing this, Eiu grows angry and glares at him. They are wrapped in a single sheet. Another prayer is said. Papa takes the sheet to Mama.

Eiu remains with the rabbits. He feels a hand squeeze his right shoulder from behind. Startled, Eiu turns quickly. An older man stands in front of him. Before Eui can figure out what to do, the man hugs him. Looking over the man's shoulder, he sees Papa returning.

Papa places his hand on Eiu's chest and says, "Eiu." Then he puts his hand on his chest and says, "Papa." He places his hand on the man's chest and says, "Mama Papa." Now Eiu understands. This man is Mama's father and my grandfather.

The two men converse in the ancestral tongue. They head back toward the house, with Eiu following behind.

Inside, the dining table has more sections than when Equo and Eiu left this morning. Two older women are sitting with Mama at the far end. Another older man is sitting next to one of the women. All three of them come over to hug him. Papa introduces them as his parents and Mama's mama. A pile of sandwiches and a large plate of raw and pickled vegetables sit in the middle of the table. Pitchers of water and glasses accompany them. Papa and Eiu wash their hands in the sink. Upon their return, everyone else rises from their seats.

Although they talk too fast for Eiu to understand everything, he catches snippets of the conversations - the bell for the Morning meal rings. Holding hands, they sing the prayer of thanksgiving in the ancestral tongue:

"Fir On, we thank you for the plants and animals you provide and the energy you give to make them healthy and strong. Please transfer that energy from them to us so we may return it to the universe positively and live in health, happiness, and harmony."

The others leave the table. They return with their copy of *The No Fir*. Eiu retrieves copies of his City Speak and ancestral tongue versions. Mama's mama says a specific passage. The rest turn to it. Mama assists Eiu with finding it in his ancestral tongue version. He also finds it in his City Speak version. Reciting the passage melodically, her mother brings a new dimension to studying. Again, Eiu doesn't understand the entire conversation, but he picks up several concepts. Utilizing both translations is beneficial.

After completing the morning Wisdom study, Mama's mama orders her, Papa, and Eiu to bed. The four grandparents will oversee the chores and watch over the animals. Suddenly, Eiu realizes just how tired he truly is. The three of them hadn't slept in more than a day. Eiu falls asleep immediately.

***

Ateq shakes Eiu awake. "Are you going to sleep through another meal and Wisdom study? Besides, coming to the kitchen before the faschnachts are gone would be best."

Eiu tries to clear the cobwebs from his head, "Faschnachts? What are they?"

"Deep-fried yeast-leavened dough buns. They are delicious. It took all my restraint not to eat them all on the way home. I have so much to tell you," Ateq replies.

Hearing this, Eiu catapults out of bed and dresses in less than a minute. The smells coming from the kitchen lead him by the nose. The grandmothers stand in front of the stove. It sounds like they are disagreeing about something. The cutting board on the table overflows with chopped vegetables. Mama picks up the stems and scraps. She hands them to Ateq. He heads out the front door to feed them to the pigs.

Eiu takes a faschnacht from the waxed paper bag. Biting into it, a big smile crosses his face. Ateq is right. These are delicious. He has never tasted anything like it.

Seeing the smile, Ateq says, "I told you so. Aren't you glad you came out here? Mama says we can only have one, so everyone can enjoy them. She says you have met our grandparents. They live in the house behind us together. With so many relatives, our grandparents spend a lot of time visiting. They came back for the birthing season. They made it just in time. The ancestral word for grandmother is Mamatu. Grandfather is Papatu. To the left is Mamatu Udon, Papa's Mama, and on the right is Mama's Mama, Mamatu Ueon. Watch out for Mamatu Udon. She bosses everyone around and corrects them harshly for the tiniest mistake. I love spending time with Mamatu Ueon. Being with her is so much fun. She likes to play games. Mamatu Udon and Papatu Otau are partners. Mamatu Ueon and Papatu Uoea are partners. Papatu Uoea doesn't like me much. He thinks Mama and Papa are too easy on me. Papatu Uoea adores Adiu. Her only mistake is being a girl. Both pairs grew up in the same orthodox community." Ateq continues, "Papa paid the local matron many colonial units to suggest he was Mama's perfect partner. They have been together for fifty-three years."

Eiu makes some calculations in his head. "How old are our parents?"

"Seventy-nine," Ateq replies.

Eiu is amazed. He struggles to keep up with them doing the chores. "So, how old are our grandparents?"

"Mamatu Udon is one hundred-fifteen years old, Papatu Otau is one hundred-seventeen years old, and Mamatu Ueon and Papatu Uoea are one hundred-twelve years old," Ateq answers

Eiu lets out a whistle. "Do homesteaders usually live this long?"

"Longer. Women live into the one hundred-eighty-year range. Men average a little less: one hundred-sixties. We also have three great-grandparents still alive. One great-grandfather and great-grandmother on Mama's side. Mamatre Eaoc and Papatre Osea, Papatu Uoea's parents. They are one hundred forty-two years old. On Papa's side, Mamatu Otau's mama, Mamatre Eatu, is one hundred fifty-one years old," Ateq says.

Eiu says, "Just a moment. I need my notebook. I am so confused. I need to write all of this down." He returns to the kitchen.

Mama and Papa's Family Tree (Year Born)
Mama Equo (2080)
　　Mamatu Ueon (2047) and Papatu Uoea (2047).
Papatu Uoea (2047)
　　Mamatre Eaoc (2017) and Papatre Osea (2017).

Papa Iuot (2080)
　　Mamatu Otau (2044) and Papatu Udon (2042).
Mamatu Otau (2044)
　　Mamatre Eatu (2008).

Ateq corrects him when necessary. Sitting there, looking at the ages, Eiu has a thought. I am thirty-nine years old. Adiu is fifty-two years old. I will have to live to the age of one hundred forty-seven if she lives until age one hundred sixty. The until-death part of the partner contract makes sense. Adiu could outlive me by many decades. She will be eighty-five if I live until my father's age of seventy-two. It puts the thirteen years to pay off my debt into perspective.

The papatus and Papa return from the barns. Each has a basket of eggs. Papa takes a long candle on a stand from a cabinet top. He places it on the table and lights it. Papa holds an egg to the flame. Mama places a large bowl next to his elbow. After staring at the egg momentarily, he places it in the large bowl. Papa continues to do this for each egg in his basket. Soon, his basket is empty. The eggs are divided into two groups: ones in the large bowl and others on the table. Papa returns the table group to his basket. He takes Papatu Uoea's basket next.

Eiu can't control his curiosity any longer. "Papa, what are you doing?"

Ateq translates his question. After listening to Papa's answer in the ancestral tongue, he translates for Eiu.

"Papa is holding the eggs up to the light to see if a chick has begun to form. We will return the egg to the brooding boxes if there is a chick. A hen will sit on the egg until it hatches. If the egg is fresh without a chick, Mama will put it in the refrigerator to be eaten. It is called candling an egg. The eggs in the large bowl are fresh. The eggs in his basket will go back to the hen house. Within a few weeks, the chicks will hatch. Papa keeps a record of the hens who are laying eggs. Once they are not laying, they are killed. The new brood of hens will replace them."

Eiu remembers his anger about Papa snapping the necks of the ill rabbit kittens. "Why did he kill the sick newborn bunnies?" he asked with his temperature rising.

"I can answer this. Rabbits can have up to four large litters each year. Up to half of a litter will die from disease, predators, or the doe refuses to care for them if they are ill. Papa is being kind by killing them as newborns. It is better than dying from disease slowly or being neglected by their mother. It also gives the healthy kittens a better chance to survive," Ateq says.

Eiu feels foolish for thinking the worst of Papa. Ateq translates the conversation for the rest of the family. Mama hugs him.

As the year progresses, Eiu learns more about the homestead and its workings. All the family works with him to understand the ancestral tongue. At harvest time, the men select the animals to be sold or slaughtered. As each chosen animal is killed, the men take a moment to thank Fir On for his blessings. The root cellars are full of vegetables, fruits, and grain sacks. Hay, straw, and animal feed fill the barns.

One day, Mama and Papa call Eiu and Ateq into the kitchen. Mama reads the total expenses, revenue, and profit for the year. She gives Ateq one-fourth of the profits, and Eiu receives one-eighth. It has been a good year. Eiu counts the colonial unit notes lying before him. He sets aside the 6,151 colonial units for his missing dowry. He asks Mama and Papa to give it to Adiu.

Then, Eiu takes ten percent for himself and gives the rest to Mama. "This belongs to you. I want you and Papa to do something nice for yourselves."

Both parents look at each other quizzically. "Why? We have everything we need," Papa says.

Eiu replies, "Use it for something you want, but you won't spend the money. Splurge. You deserve more than just your needs."

Ateq slaps him on the back. Mama and Papa smile, but tears well up in their eyes. "Are you trying to make me look bad?" Ateq asks.

Chapter 17

The day after Ateu's departure, the hydroelectric company installs water wheels along the stream. The supervisor explains to Adiu how the system works. "Each water wheel has rustproof steel blades that slightly enter the water. Each blade is attached to a small turbine. A long rod runs through the center of the turbine, crossing the stream. The rod attaches to two electric generators: one atop each side of the concrete culvert. The water spins the blades of the turbine. As the turbine and attached rod spin, the generators also spin. The created electricity travels through wires to storage batteries. The batteries supply the electricity through wires as needed. Your circulation fan and lights will use this electricity. The larger water wheel of the grain mill will supplement the smaller systems. It will also spin the gears of the grinding stones. With the constant speed of the stream, you will have a regular supply of electricity. The electricity will be directed to your backup battery system when the storage batteries are full. The entire system will shut down when there is more electricity than the batteries can hold until the batteries reach seventy-five percent capacity. Then, the system will turn itself back on. There is a manual override backup." Adiu learned about hydroelectric systems in Secondary school, but seeing them in action reinforced her choice of the electrical production system.

A steel building company will construct the grain mill. A local quarry will supply the grinding stones. An electrical inspector will meet with Adiu and the supervisors of each company to approve their work or make suggestions. Once the system receives certification, there will be lights and air circulation. This system and the construction costs for the buildings are most of Adiu's expenses. Her parents could have their well system retrofitted to use hydroelectric, but there is a risk of damage to the old pipes, and the cost outweighs the benefit they would receive. Adiu crosses the concrete bridge to watch the installation of a concave dome above the cavern. The installation company's supervisor explains the process to her. "They fit the dome and its reflective panels at a forty-five-degree angle. The panels will reflect sunlight toward the dome, and the dome's concavity will disperse the light outward, covering a large portion of the cavern. The railroad company uses these to provide light along its rails. The domes don't affect the ability of the trains to move through the vacuum tunnels."

Returning to the construction site, Adiu inspects several large square bamboo frames near the matting crew. On each side, poles run through rings of bamboo matting. Two opposite poles are twelve feet high, and the perpendicular poles are sixteen feet long. A natural opaque sealant covers the poles and mat walls.

Room Layout Plan (Left to Right)

Bathroom (One Outside Door, Three 12-foot × 16-foot Walls, One 12-foot × 12-foot Vertical Wall)

Second Bed Chamber (One Inside Door, Two 12-foot × 16-foot Walls, One 12-foot × 12-foot Wall)

Sitting Room (Two Outside Doors, One 12-foot × 16-foot Wall, One 12-foot × 8-foot Wall)

Kitchen/Dining Area (Entranceway, One 12-foot × 16-foot Wall, One 12-foot × 12-foot Wall)

First Bed Chamber (Inside Door, Three 12-foot × 16-foot, One 12-foot × 12-foot Wall)

Total Wall Square Footage: 2,592 sq. ft.
Total Square Footage: 16 feet wide × 80 feet long
1,280 sq. ft.

According to the blueprint Adiu is reading, there will be fifteen 12-foot x 16-foot walls, four 12-foot x 12-foot walls, and one 12-foot x 8-foot wall.

A ceiling fan/light combination will illuminate and provide air circulation for each room. Lard lamps will supply additional light when needed.

Adiu's building contract guarantees no additional expenses if she pays in cash with a twenty-five percent deposit. Oasi also gave her a discount for her cash payment.

Oasi Family Construction - House Quote
Adiu Equo Iuot

Bamboo Wall Construction
(Materials & Labor): 2,592 Square Feet x 13 colonial units/foot: **33,696 colonial units**

Straw & Adobe Application
(Materials & Labor): 5,184 Square Feet x 13 colonial units/foot: **67,392 colonial units**

Total Estimate: **101,088 colonial units**
Minus Cash Discount: **-10,109 colonial units**

Final Cost: **90,979 colonial units**

Deep in thought, it took a throat clearing to get her attention. Turning, the dome installation supervisor stands waiting. "We have finished. Please come look." Adiu follows. The supervisor signals a crew member standing at the top of the scaffolding. He pulls a large cover, allowing the sunlight to fill the cavern. All work ceases, and there is absolute silence. Looking up, everyone is shading their eyes from the brightness. A round of applause resounds from the cavern walls. Adiu joins the rest in their appreciation of their work. Adiu hugs the supervisor, who is surprised by her response. Once his composure is restored, the supervisor says, "Now comes the less pleasant part: the bill." He follows Adiu back to the table. She reviews the bill:

Schmidt Family Dome Lighting Company
Client: Adiu Equo Iuot

One 39 Square Foot Concave Dome & Reflective Panel Unit (Materials & Labor):

19,773.00 colonial units

Minus **25% Railroad Discount**:

- 4,943.25 colonial units

Minus **10% Cash Discount**: **- 1,977.30 colonial units**

Final Cost: **12,832.45 colonial units**

"Tell your mother I will be in her office tomorrow with the payment. Thank you so much for such excellent work. Please take this for you and your crew. It is just a little token of my appreciation," Adiu says, handing him a sealed envelope.

"We can't. Your thanks are enough," the supervisor replies, trying to return the envelope.

"I insist," Adiu says, refusing to accept it.

"My crew and I appreciate your generosity."

Turning back to the table, Adiu writes the amount of the gift in her ledger: 1,000 colonial units. It has been a busy and exciting day. Her clock rings at 10:00, and the crews clean up before heading home for the evening.

***

Sitting with her meal by the fire, Adiu reflects upon the day. It has been a good day. It is this time of the evening when she misses Eiu the most. She includes him and her family in her prayers. Before retiring, Adiu takes two carrots to the horses in their makeshift corral. Rubbing their necks, they neigh their approval of the treat.

Only two crews arrive to work the next day. For those living in Fertility, it is the Sabbath. On the Sabbath, they attend church services and spend the day resting and reading *Di Heilich Shrift*. With all the businesses closed for the day, Adiu decides to mark out the locations for the crops. She borrows a piece of chalk to mark them on the ground. She has a rough sketch on paper to follow.

Cavern Left Wall

Aisle 1 - Row 1: 2 Potato, 1 Sweet Potato, 1 Carrot, Row 2: 1 Parsnip & Turnips, 1 Kohlrabi & Radishes, 1 Beans, 1 Peas, Row 3: 1 Onions, 1 Scallion, Shallot & Leeks, 1 Beets, 1 Cabbage & Endive, Row 4: 1 Broccoli & Cauliflower, 1 Lettuce,1 Sprouts & Asparagus, 1 Kale & Spinach, Row 5: 1 Celery & Peppers, 1 Radicchio & Rhubarb, 1 Garlic & Ginger, 1 Turmeric & Fennel, Row 6: 1 Pumpkin & Cucumber, 1 Squash & Zucchini, 1 Eggplant & Watermelon, 1 Cantaloupe & Honeydew

Aisle 2 - Rows 1 & 2: Black Grapes, Rows 3 & 4: Red Grapes, Rows 5 & 6: Green Grapes

Aisle 3 - Row 1 & 2: Large Tomatoes, Row 3 & 4: Medium Tomatoes, Row 5 & 6: Small Tomatoes

Aisle 4 - Rows 1 & 2: Black Cherries, Rows 3 & 4: Red Apples, Rows 5 & 6: Green Apples

Aisle 5 - Row 1 & 2: Peaches, Row 3 & 4: Pears, Row 5 & 6: Figs

Aisle 6 - Row 1 & 2: Tangerines, Row 3 & 4: Apricots, Row 5 & 6: Lemons

Aisle 7 - Row 1: 2 Red Raspberries & 2 Black Raspberries, Row 2: 2 Blueberries & 2 Blackberries, Row 3: Strawberries, Row 4: 1 Gooseberry, 1 Mulberry, 1 Snowberry, & 1 Thimbleberry, Row 5: 1 Lingonberry, 1 Pawpaw, 1 Bilberry, & 1 Chokeberry, Row 6: 1 Red Currant, 1 Black Currant, 1 Huckleberry, & 1 Elderberry

---

On the left side of the stream, the fruit and vegetables will be planted in the corner nearest the entrance. She marks four 4-foot x 8-foot rectangles in six rows with labels perpendicular to the front cavern wall, leaving space around each to move. Grapes and tomatoes will grow in perpendicular rows half the width of the area allotted to the animal troughs for vegetables.

After she finishes marking each location, Adiu draws a 3-foot diameter circle from the mark for the fruit trees. This marks the width of the circle she must dig for each tree. The Midday Meal bell rings. While eating, Adiu thinks about a day of rest. Homesteaders work daily because they have animals and crops that require constant attention. When one crop is harvested, there is a cleanup period to prepare the ground for the next. Crop rotation helps the soil but requires meticulous planning. I like the idea of taking some time off, but only a part of the day. I have things I could do this afternoon, but I want to see what it is like just to read and rest. I will read *The No Fir.*

***

Adiu receives a telegram the following morning at the mail delivery building. Her Mamatus and Papatus are stopping by. She must pick them up in Intercourse, the closest town with a train station. They will arrive before the Midday Meal and stay until one of Adiu's cousins picks them up before the Evening Meal. This news changes her plans. The mail agent, Jakob, gives her directions to the train station and tells her how long the trip is. Adiu leaves the mail delivery office, heading south out of town. She will have about an hour to wait for their train to arrive if they are on time.

The ride back to Fertility is filled with everyone wanting to know everything. When they arrive, it is Midday Meal time. Adiu leads her elders to the community restaurant. When Ateq returned, he talked about the menu in great detail. They are all excited to try it. Adiu explains to their server whom she has with her. The server seats them and leaves the group to talk for a few minutes. Upon her return, the server brings pitchers of water, coffee, and iced tea to the table. Three more servers bring large plates of food. No more do they place them on the table; the servers return with more. Their server explains what is on each plate and how it is made. Adiu translates her words into the ancestral tongue. Her mamatus and papatus take a small portion of each item as the plates are passed around the table. Adiu watches their faces as they eat. The mamatus and papatus go back for seconds and thirds of the items they like. If a plate is empty, another full one takes its place. The group is silent throughout the meal. This never happens at home. Adiu looks at each of them; they are too busy eating to talk. When her elders have had enough of an item, they shake their hands sideways over the plate to indicate this. A large desert tray appears when belts are loosened, and bellies are rubbed. A slice of each type of cake or pie is placed on the table. These are cut into pieces for everyone to share. The server asks if there is anything they need. Adiu asks the others. All heads shake in a negative response. While the others visit the bathrooms, she pays the bill and gives each server a tip. Boarding the wagon, they head to Adiu's homestead.

They know Oasi's and Ieoc's families, so they take time to talk with them as Adiu gives them a tour. She explains how the hydroelectric system works. They are still discussing different facets of the homestead when Adiu's cousin arrives. They have a long trip ahead, so the mamatus and papatus quickly make their farewells. Adiu follows the wagon as far as the end of the underground exit. Shortly, the crews begin gathering their tools and materials. She doesn't build a fire but goes straight to bed. Six months into the project, Adiu is looking over her task list. She checks off those that are completed:

✔ *1. Oasi's sons and grandchildren construct the house.*
✔ *2. Ioec lay the floors.*
✔ *3. The barns need to be dug.*
✔ *4. Install a hydroelectric system.*
✔ *5. Install a dome lighting system.*
✔ *6. Construct a grain mill and water wheel connected to an electrical system.*
✔ *7. Install ceiling fan/light combinations in each room and building.*
✔ *8. Plant the vegetables, fruit trees, and berry bushes.*
✔ *9. Purchase a small wagon and six billy goats to pull it.*
✔ *10. Purchase canning supplies.*

✔ *11. Purchase straw bales for the root cellar.*

✔ *12. Purchase feed for the goats.*

13. Move things from the yurt into the house. Ateq is coming to assist.

14. Install the electric stove. Oasi's sons are bringing her stove with a warmer above the burners next week.

15. Rototill the rows for planting grain seeds. Naomi's husband will lend a rototiller.

16. Weave baskets and netting for the fruit and vegetables

17. Gather the fruit and vegetables when ripe.

18. Can fresh fruit and vegetables.

19. Make jams, jellies, marmalades, and preserves.

20. Can fermented vegetables: pickles, carrots, cauliflower, and cabbage.

✔ *21. Fencing and gates for animal enclosures and barns.*

Adiu is pleased with the amount of work she was able to accomplish. Digging the 3-foot diameter holes for the fruit trees by hand took longer than Adiu had planned. Carrying the small stones, manure, and soil from their piles by wheelbarrow to the forty-eight animal trough vegetable and berry beds took almost a month. Adiu fills buckets from the hand pump daily and waters all the crops.

After the evening meal, she enjoys sitting beside the fire, reading *The No Fir* and *Di Heilich Shrift*. In her notebook, Adiu writes the similarities and differences between the two belief systems. She finds the concepts of original sin and salvation fascinating.

Chapter 18

Ateq arrives at the train station in Intercourse. On their way back, Adiu and Ateq discuss what is happening at their parents' homestead.

Ateq says, "The birthing season went well. Our Mamatus and Papatus make taking care of the newborns easier. The amount of loss is lower than average. You will have a large number of animals."

"How is Eiu?" Adiu asked.

"The death part is difficult for him. Everyone works with him to learn the ancestral tongue. Staring at him and making faces has become Momma's latest reprimand method when Eiu makes mistakes or doesn't understand. He spent several days with bandages on his hands until his callouses hardened. Weekly, Mama and Eiu write down a schedule of chores. She makes him write it in the ancestral tongue. You should see Eiu's working muscles." Ateq flexes his right arm muscles.

Adiu smacks him on the back of the head. "Does he say anything about his feelings?" she asks.

"Oh, you want to know if Eiu still cares." Ateq winks at his sister. "Not a bit. Eiu is working too hard to have the time or the energy for such frivolous things." Seeing the sadness in her eyes, Ateq stops teasing Adiu. "Eiu prays for you at least five times a day. He asks so many questions when I return from here and wants me to tell him all the details." A smile replaces the sadness. Adiu smacks Ateq again for teasing her.

"Are you hungry? We can go to the restaurant before going to the homestead," says Adiu.

"When was the last time I wasn't hungry?" Ateq retorts.

They make another stop, the mail delivery office. Jakob greets Ateq by name.

***

Seeing all the completed work, Ateq greatly admires Adiu. This was challenging to do and took a long time to complete. Adiu and

Ateq load the bedroom items into the wagon and unload them at the front double doors of the house. Entering through the two open doors makes the transition easier. Next, the kitchen and dining area furniture are placed in designated locations. The job is complete with the sitting room furniture. Adiu and Ateq flop down on the tufted sitting room chairs, taking a moment to catch their breaths.

"Let me give you a tour before we go to the mercantile for the order I placed," Adiu says to Ateq. Walking around, they notice some fruit and vegetables ready to be harvested. "The canning will need to be done with the cauldron since the electric stove will not be available until next week," Adiu says.

At the mercantile, Adiu introduces Ateq to Moses. He and his wife, Sarah, moved to Fertility five years ago to take over when her uncle Aaron, the previous owner, passed away. Ateq knows the story of the thirteen original couples created by the Fir On. Each couple was of a different race and was sent to various locations in the First Planet. He didn't know this also occurred in those with other beliefs, so Ateq is surprised to meet a dark-skinned couple in Fertility. Even among the orthodox communities, there is rarely a mix of different races. Ateq has so many questions. Moses leads them to the loading dock at the back of the store. While Adiu and Moses review her shopping list, Ateq goes out front to bring the buggy to the back. Canning jars, lids, a metal can tong, two canning jar racks, two canning pots with lids, gallons of vinegar, a bag of yeast, sugar, and pickling spices fill the trunk and the back of the buggy. Adiu pays her bill at the front register. Sarah comes down the stairs with a baby in her arms. Adiu asks to hold Nehemiah. Ateq looks around the mercantile. Seeing his sister holding the baby makes him sad. Adiu will never know what it is like to have a child. Just then, Ateq's gaze lands on a pair of strange-looking boots. They don't have a stiff sole. Instead, they are entirely made of leather. They are very long and would lace up to just below his knees.

"All-natural boots made in Paradise. Feet and toes stretch out. The wearer feels ground. Last long time. Can be patched," Moses says from behind him.

"They are also waterproof," Adiu added. "I was initially skeptical, but Sarah told me about her pair, and I just had to try them. I wear mine all the time. See," Adiu lifts her skirt. "Would you like a pair?" she asks.

"Are you sure?" Ateq asks.

"Moses, will you please help him find a pair? Sarah, will you add the cost to my account? I will stop by later this week to pay for them," Adiu asks. "He will also need four pairs of long socks."

Ateq arrives at Adiu's buggy with a bag holding his work boots and three pairs of long socks. Walking in the parking lot requires Ateq to adjust to feeling the different materials with his feet and toes.

"Moses says I can also tuck my pants into the boots. They will not get wet unless I go into deep water," Ateq says. "Are Moses and his family the only non-light-skinned people in Fertility?"

"No, there are families from several different racial backgrounds. Like our community, they were removed from the Beta and relocated here. The Universal Alliance government chose to place them all between two mountain ranges. There is the one where several other Orthodox Homestead families and I live and a second one just over three hundred-ninety miles west. Many of their ancestors lived underground when they first arrived. However, by pooling their resources, communities could purchase thirty-nine square mile domes, like the one that covers Fertility. Underground roads connect these communities. To supply the needs of each community, the people who produce materials and provide services agree to move where they are needed. So, each community is a mix of people from different races," Adiu informs Ateq.

***

As they eat lunch at the restaurant, Adiu notices that the same young lady serves them again. The restaurant has many serving staff.

What are the chances that their server will ask to take their table each time Ateq is here? Has he noticed? Should I tell him? Adiu wonders.

Once they return to the homestead, Adiu and Ateq move the long tables near the cauldron and carry buckets of water from the hand pump to fill it. Unloading the canning supplies onto the tables, they work together to sterilize the jars and lids once the cauldron water boils. The tables are covered with rolls of waxed sheeting. Submerging the two loaded canning jar racks in the water, timing them, removing the jars and lids needed to preserve the ripe fruit and vegetables, and placing them onto the covered tables takes up the remainder of the day. A second layer of sheeting will keep the items clean until the morning.

After the Morning Meal and Wisdom studies, Ateq retrieves the ripe fruit from the trees. Adiu carries the cooled water from the cauldron and pours it into the stream. They fill buckets with cool water and place them on the benches near the tables. The ripe fruit is poured from the woven baskets into the water to be cleaned. Scrubbing the individual pieces of fruit, Adiu and Ateq carefully rub the crocheted cleaning pad against its skin. The cleaned fruit is piled on towels, waiting their turn to be jam, jelly, or preserves. The dirty water is carried to the stream once all the vegetables and fruit are bathed. Another fire burns under the cauldron; this time, the embers are raked out to heat slower and evenly. Constant stirring is required until the fruit, honey, and water mixture becomes the correct consistency in the cauldron.

Ateq leaves Adiu to finish filling the glass jars and screwing down the lids and rings. His task for the day is tilling the ground for the grain seeds. Using the borrowed rototiller, Ateq furrows long lines in the designated area. He carries wheelbarrow loads of manure from a pile, changing the location from light brown to dark chocolate. Another tilling of the soil and manure leaves the area looking like brownies with caramel swirls. Ateq is hot, sweaty, and dirty. He strips to his underwear and enters the stream just before the first spinning water wheels of the hydroelectric system. Adiu sees his fair skin reappear as Ateq washes.

"I have finished canning for the day and cleaned the cauldron. I will get some warm water started. You can take a proper bath," Adiu says.

"That will be wonderful. I forgot what it is like doing actual manual labor. Please remind me to kiss the farm tractor when I get back," Ateq replied.

Ateq strips and pours warm water over his arms, chest, and head. The environmentally safe soap bar rubs against the natural bath sponge. After Ateq dresses, they head to the community restaurant for the Evening Meal.

Will the same woman serve us tonight? I am glad he is bathing before going out. She doesn't wear her hair under a covering.

Does she not believe in God? What would happen if Ateq caught on? What would he do? Adiu wonders.

Adiu is so deep in thought about Ateq that he successfully snaps the towel against her butt. Turning around to scold him, she sees the beginning of a mustache and beard. Grabbing his face, Adiu says, "I think you missed your upper lip and the area around your chin."

"You are so funny. I am forty years old, but I have a baby face. Women don't take me seriously. They call me a boy," Ateq says.

"Have you thought it may be your actions, not your face, that leads them to believe you are younger?" Adiu teases.

"It is easy for you. You are a woman. Women have all the power: the right to choose their partners, be the head of the household, receive larger portions of inheritance whether they are firstborn or not, and be given more opportunities based on gender. You have no idea what it is like to compete for the attention of a suitable partner," Ateq says.

"My poor brother," says Adiu, "You may have to stay at home, eating Mama's food, sleeping under the blankets Mama quilts, wearing the clothes Mama makes, and being cared for by Mama and Papa. Besides, you have lived this long without a woman, so if we are so bad, you should leave us for other men who find us wonderful."

The siblings' verbal jabs continue until they arrive at the restaurant. Adiu opens the door and a young girl races toward the kitchen. The double doors swing behind their regular server. A smile grows across the server's face when she sees Adiu's meal companion. Adiu walks forward toward a table in the back. She thinks this situation reminds me of picture puzzles with the object of finding the differences. Once you see it, you can't stop seeing it. Unable to see this may be the reason Ateq is still single.

***

After the Morning Meal and Wisdom studies, Ateq takes the horses and wagon home the next day. A thought crosses Ateq's mind just as he is prepared to leave: I will return in about six months with Adiu's inheritance. The Papatus, Papa, and I will use all four wagons. Mama will decide if Eiu will come. He keeps this to himself—no need to give Adiu hope, only to have her heart broken if Mama says no.

Adiu finishes canning the fruit before the Midday Meal. The afternoon's task consists of canning the ripe vegetables: carrots, beans, peas, beets, broccoli, cauliflower, rhubarb, eggplant, sprouts, and asparagus. This work will be finished the next day. Sitting in front of the fire after her Evening Meal and Wisdom studies, Adiu reviews her task checklist:

✓ 1. *Oasi's sons and grandchildren construct the house.*

✓ 2. *Ioec lay the floors.*

✓ 3. *The barns need to be dug.*

✓ 4. *Install a hydroelectric system.*

✓ 5. *Install a dome lighting system.*

✓ 6. *Construct a grain mill and water wheel connected to an electrical system.*

✓ 7. *Install ceiling fan/light combinations in each room and building.*

✓ 8. *Plant the vegetables, fruit trees, and berry bushes.*

✓ 9. *Purchase a small wagon and six billy goats to pull it.*

✓ 10. *Purchase canning supplies.*

✓ 11. *Purchase straw bales for the root cellar.*

✓ 12. *Purchase feed for the goats.*

✓ 13. *Move things from the yurt into the house. Ateq is coming to assist.*

14. *Install the electric stove. Oasi's sons are bringing her stove with a warmer above the burners next week.*

✓ 15. *Rototill the rows for planting grain seeds. Naomi's husband will lend a rototiller.*

✓ 16. *Weave baskets and netting for the fruit and vegetables*

✓ 17. *Gather the fruit and vegetables when ripe.*

✓ 18. *Can fresh fruit and vegetables.*

✓ 19. *Make jams, jellies, marmalades, and preserves.*

20. *Can fermented vegetables: pickles, carrots, cauliflower, and cabbage.*

✓ 21. *Fencing and gates for animal enclosures and barns.*

Arriving at the mail delivery office, Adiu sees seven teams of horses and canvas-covered wagons tied to the railing. She considers the household goods and tools inside one of the wagons. The mail agent, Jakob, is talking to several men at his desk. Listening to the strangers talking, Adiu doesn't understand them. Their language sounds like a combination of City Speak, the ancestral tongue, and the language of the townspeople. The men and boys wear black cotton suits, including a coat, vest, and pants. Their white, collared shirts peak out. Black top hats cover their heads, with their hair cut straight just above the top of their ears. The women and girls wear black coats, aprons, and tights. Black bonnets cover their heads and block their faces at the side. All the women's and girls' dresses are dark, solid colors. After the group leaves the building, Adiu asks, "New Neighbors?"

"Yes, Purchased twenty-six square miles to west. Don't talk to outsiders. Come to town for deliveries and mail. Given nine months to leave. Drove wagons from the east. Walked over mountains. Trip took ten months. Expelled 'cause refused give up their beliefs, like us," Jakob responds.

Each day slides into the next, causing Adiu to forget which day it is. One morning, in particular, Adiu heads into Fertility. Leaving the underground entrance, she realizes no business will be conducted today. The roads are empty, and the businesses are closed. It is the Sabbath. Thinking of things to do instead, Adiu looks toward the west. She thinks I haven't gone outside of Fertility in that direction. Maybe I will see our new neighbors.

Heading out of the downtown area, Adiu sees miles of fields surrounding compounds of buildings. Each driveway has a large metal sign with the family name and services they provide. There are lights outside and inside the buildings, but the electrical poles and wires are missing.

How do they get their electricity? The answer comes when she looks behind the buildings. Giant windmills attached to steel buildings spin. The wires must be buried underground.

That is interesting. In town, there is a community electrical company with solar panels. Poles rise at the street corners, and wires are strung between them. Each house has electrical boxes with a wire from the main line.

***

Twenty miles outside Fertility, the gravel and pitch road ends. Adiu sees the canvas-covered wagons lined up along a distant, perpendicular dirt road. To the north, seven smaller wagons are hitched to single horses facing the road. The wagons are just like hers.

Adiu's wagon is a black square box with an opening for the driver's seat and windows in doors on each side. It has two bench seats for six people and a deep trunk in the back to haul things.

A battery is under the back seat for the lights and turn signals. It also has a sizable reflective triangle on the back of the trunk so people can see the wagon at night. Her wagon is called a buggy. Adiu observes that their buggies do not have headlights or turn signals.

Watching people move around the wagons, Adiu wants to continue until the end of the westward road. The buck goats are great for local tasks, but she is still determining how far they can go without tiring too much. Sighing, Adiu clicks her tongue and pulls the right rein. It is getting late anyway. Leading the bucks to their barn, Adiu rubs their necks and tells them how much she appreciates their hard work. Adiu goes to the apple trees for six apples to treat the goats. It takes focus to ensure each goat gets only one apple because the bucks push each other out of the way. Bleats of appreciation meet Adiu's ears on her way back to her house.

For the next seven months, Adiu spends her days gathering vegetables, fruit, and berries. The grains grow taller, including oats, bran, rice, wheat, quinoa, barley, millet, buckwheat, bulgur, rye, sorghum, and spelt. Rows of animal feed grasses also grow.

Chapter 19

Adiu's Next Six Years
2160 to 2166

Adiu celebrates her first year on her homestead by eating lunch at the community restaurant. After her meal, she sees Moses unloading boxes and returning with different boxes. She waves to him and says, "Hello!" He looks busy and solemn, so Adiu decides not to bother him.

At the mail delivery office, Adiu receives a telegram from Mama:

Lancaster Telegram & Telephone Co.

From: Equo Udon Udos
To: Adiu Equo Iuot

*There is a break in the work. I am sending your inheritance.
The four men loaded up your equipment and animals. They leave this
morning. They should arrive in three to four days. Your Papatus,
Papa, and Ateq can stay for the grain harvest.*
Mama

Adiu is excited to receive the equipment and animals. Unlike the fruit and vegetables, which can wait to be harvested, the grain fields can't. Adiu was planning their harvest for next week, thinking they would be dry enough by then. Then, a thought hit her. Eiu isn't coming. Mama said it would only take a year for him to pay his debt for breaking the partnership contract. Ateq said they had an above-average harvest, so Eiu should be able to pay me. But what if Eiu doesn't want to pay me? By not paying his debt, Eiu isn't able to be my partner. Maybe Eiu is happy without me. He has a mama, a papa, and a brother who love him. Eiu may no longer want a partner. Maybe he wants a different partner? Did Eiu ask not to come?

"Anything else?" Jakob asks.

Snapping out of her self-centered thoughts, Adiu asks, "How are the newcomers out west doing?"

"Not well. Plows not right. Refuse rototillers 'cause have engines. Traveling supplies for trip, no room for tools," he replies.

"I thought they don't talk to anyone outside their community. How did you find out?" she asks.

"Doc Masterson goes for care and records."

"Why didn't you tell me?" Adiu asks.

The mail agent says, "You have homestead. You are alone."

"Really? It is very kind of you to worry, but I have done this work all my life. The most difficult part was breaking new ground for the grain fields. Using the rototiller made Ateq's job easier. So, I understand their struggles. What can I do to help?"

"Restaurant sending food. Moses and Sarah bought sew machines, fabric, and such. Delivered last week. Fertility families gather extra clothes," he replied.

"My family left this morning to bring equipment and animals for my homestead. They should arrive in the next three to four days. I will let you know when my family arrives. Moses can come over to get what the Western community can use. In the meantime, I know what they need to plow their fields. Homesteaders use a double-sided steel plow with handles. A team of four horses pulls it. I have one coming. They can use it. I will ask my mama where we purchased ours."

"Not happy about help. 'specially from others, but need. Doc going out later today," Jakob says.

"Thank you for the information. Tell everyone to stop worrying about me so much," Adiu says as she walks out the front door.

***

Adiu heads out of town on the western road. Just before it turns to gravel, she remembers seeing a steel sign with Malachi Masterson, MD, on the left side of the road. Upon her arrival, another sign in the driveway directs people to his office in the basement. The doctor's office door is locked. Adiu heads to the first-floor front door and rings the doorbell. "Hello, help you?" a small child asks.

"Is Dr. or Mrs. Masterson available? I am Adiu Equo Iuot. I live near the town," she replies.

"No, Mrs. Doc dead. Get Doc."

Adiu waits patiently on the sidewalk. No, Mrs. Masterson? Is that child the doctor's daughter? Why does she refer to him as Doc?

A tall, slender man arrives at the open door. "Hello, I am Dr. Masterson, but everyone calls me Doc. May I help you?" he asks.

"I am here to help you. I am Adiu Equo Iuot. I live under the mountain east of town. Jakob says the Fertility community is helping our neighbors to the west. You may call me Adiu," she

182

says, pointing in that direction. "I have completed my first harvest. I want to donate."

"That is very nice of you. Why haven't we met before?" Doc asks.

"I haven't needed the services of a doctor before," Adiu responds. "What do they need?"

Doc says, "The townspeople have given as much as possible, but this has been challenging for them. This year, the time of the darker of the binary sun's rotation is the longest in its cycle. That results in fewer days of growth with weaker sunlight. As does the weather, these rotational changes significantly impact food production and animal growth. Everyone stores reserves when times are good, but a drought several years ago required them to use part of those backup supplies. They sacrifice their own needs to help. Anything you can spare will reduce the amount needed by those in the western settlement. Also, reducing the amount the people Fertility feel obligated to give."

"I live underground and only use sunlight to support my hydro electrical and water wheel systems. How can I get food to you? I don't have any large wagons right now, but my family will arrive in three to four days with four large wagons and teams for transport." Adiu asks.

Doc says, "If you would be willing to drop off the food with Moses and Sarah, they will bring it with the other donations."

"Thank you for telling me about the townspeople. How can I help them? They have been so good to me. Anything they need that I have is theirs," Adiu says.

"Just helping out with the others is enough right now."

Adiu asks, "Can I still get food to you tonight?"

"Moses and Sarah come here after they close the mercantile. Check with them," Doc says.

Adiu says, "I will. Please let me know what else is needed, including for the people of Fertility." After shaking hands and saying their goodbyes, Adiu directs her goats toward the mercantile.

***

Adiu's menfolk arrive in two days. She prepares food boxes as Papatu Udon's team leads the convoy into the front yard. Papatu Uoea's team is next, and Papa's team follows. Eiu's team is bringing up the rear. Adiu doesn't see this immediately. A hug from Papatu Udon engulfs her. Papatu Uoea and Papa block Adiu's view, waiting for their turns. Papa turns her around so she can see over his shoulder. It is not until Adiu opens her eyes that she becomes aware that Ateq isn't standing before her. She races to Eiu but stops short. Looking back at her papa, he nods his approval.

Papa says, "Let's go clean up before we unload."

"How was your journey?" Adiu asks.

184

"It was long," Eiu says.

"Would you like to take a tour?" she asks.

"Yes," he stutters. Adiu leads him around the cavern, explaining each section in detail. Eiu is amazed by everything he sees and asks questions.

Upon returning to the wagons, Adiu and Eiu enter the house to find the others. They sit at the dining table, drinking coffee and discussing their trip.

"Are you hungry? Papatus, I want to take Papa and Eiu to the community restaurant," Adiu says in the ancestral tongue.

The Papatus tell Papa about their experience.

Papa says, "Let's go already."

The wait staff greets the Papatus like they were in only yesterday. Papa asks questions as each plate arrives at their table. Adiu tells him the name, and the Papatus give their thoughts about them. When it arrives, Papatu Udon and Papatu Uoea fight over the check.

***

The group walks down the street to the mail delivery building. Adiu introduces Jakob to her family. Their final stop is the mercantile. Moses is sweeping the front porch when they arrive. The men shake hands. Moses leads them inside. Papa and the Papatus look around at the different items for sale. Adiu overhears a discussion in the boot area. Papa is holding up a pair of boots like the ones Adiu and Ateq wear. Moses comes up behind them. Papa hands him a piece of paper with numbers on it. Looking over his shoulder, Adiu knows what Papa wants.

"Moses, my family wants boots like Ateq's and mine. The numbers on the paper are the sizes needed for my mama and grandmothers. Can you help them? Is Sara available? I want to talk to her about something," Adiu says.

Moses says, "Absolutely. Sara and the baby upstairs. Go behind counter and take stairs. I will call."

Sara is rocking the baby in the sitting room. "Sara, I discovered that the townspeople are assisting the people on the western road. I also know they are doing this at their own expense. I have the means to help. Everyone is so kind to me. I want to return the favor without making anyone feel uncomfortable. I need your advice," Adiu says.

"Appreciate considering our feelings. Difference between helping others and accepting help. Proud people embarrassed if others knew about need. I have way for you," Sara says.

Adiu asks, "What is your idea?"

"Bring things there. Moses and I tells others enough food. We give extra sometimes. We provide things to the townspeople. Not first time we help this way. Restaurant giving made food," says Sara.

Adiu says, "That explains what I saw the other day. Moses was taking boxes into the restaurant and coming out with new boxes."

"Doc and Moses leave boxes on driveways; Westerners leave empty boxes. They are good people but proud," Sara says.

Adiu asks, "If my papa and grandfathers wanted to give them a robust steel tiller to break up the soil and show them how to use it, how would they do that?"

"I ask Doc tonight," Sara says.

***

Once back at her homestead, Adiu explains the issue her neighbors are facing. The men will do anything they can to help. Later that day, Papa and the papatus take a wagon with food to the mercantile, which allows Adiu and Eiu to talk alone.

Eiu says, "Papa talked to Mama about allowing me to come in Ateq's place. I don't know what he said, but he woke me up and told me to pack a bag. I didn't ask questions. I have something for you. After the harvest was gathered and the expenses paid, Ateq and I received our portions of the profits. I earned enough to pay my debt to you. Here it is."

"Thank you for this. I wasn't sure you wanted to do this. According to *The No Fir*, I had to ask for compensation, but I knew it would not be easy. This payment frees you to enter another partnership contract," Adiu replies.

"This does cover the amount of my dowry obligation, but it does not include all your expenses. When I met with Matron about my debt, I promised her I would pay back the entire amount. She told me it would take about thirteen years. I made a promise, and I will fulfill it. I can only hope you are willing to wait. If not, I understand. I will still honor my obligation."

"Eiu, nothing has changed for me. I want to be your partner. I appreciate your promise and your willingness to fulfill it. You have met your financial obligation to me. I will wait as long as you want," Adiu says. Eiu slides his hand across the table and gently touches her fingers, resting his fingers on them. They hear the others returning. Adiu and Eiu get up from the table and enter the yard in front of the house. During the remainder of the evening, they discuss plans for harvesting the grain area.

The men use scythes to cut down the tall stalks near the ground. Giant bundles of stalks litter the area. When they whip small bundles of stalks against the sifting table, the grains fall into sacks below. The chopped stalks on a large table provide animal feed and bedding. Adiu translates Papa's instructions for Eiu. She carries the full bags with the wheelbarrow to their designated barns. She completes chores and fills out the animals' records while waiting for the subsequent sacks. There are sheep, goats, rabbits, pigs, and chickens. Adiu chose not to have cattle or horses. Each evening, the men take new supplies to the mercantile.

***

Five days later, Adiu receives a message from Doc Masterson. The men of the Western Road community will accept the tiller and instructions from her papatus. He will accompany them to translate. She is so happy that they have chosen her grandfathers. Both men will take the time to show them everything they need to know in detail, including how to maintain and repair the tiller. It is a matter of great respect for her elders. Until after planting, Her papatus travel daily to the community. Adiu creates a book of heirloom seeds for them. Finally, Papa and Eiu finish harvesting the grains. The packed sacks fill the barns.

During their Wisdom studies, Eiu utilizes both translations of *The No Fir*. Adiu is impressed with his knowledge of the ancestral tongue and the concepts covered. She worried he would not take his studies seriously, but their family is working diligently with him, and it is showing. He struggles with speaking ancestral tongue, although he can understand the readings using their context.

The day comes for the men to return to her parents' homestead. With the understanding between Adiu and Eiu, saying goodbye is easier. Papa tells Adiu he will talk to Mama about letters and telegrams between them. Adiu receives her first letter from Eiu the following week. Mama permits one letter per week. Eiu and Ateq will travel for the birthing and planting seasons. This routine continues for the next six years. Adiu continues contributing food for the people on the western road until they have two successful harvests. She also gives newborn animals when their barns are ready. Eventually, the townspeople didn't need her assistance either. Although the work is tiring, she finds great satisfaction in it.

Chapter 20

Eiu's Next Six Years & The Blight of 2166
2160 to 2166

After leaving Adiu's homestead for the first time, Eiu drives his team at the end of the convoy. His horses follow without much guidance, which is good as his thoughts are elsewhere. Eiu doesn't like the rate of death and disease among the rabbit kittens.

Eiu continues his work to increase the survival rate, even though the rabbits have large litters up to four times a year. A butcher in Lewis, a nearby town, pays him well for his grown rabbits. He likes that Eiu raises non-genetically modified animals with natural diets. Mama uses the fur for coats, gloves, hats, slippers, and meat for stews. Fortunately, there are more grown rabbits than the family needs. Most orthodox homesteaders find they can raise enough for their needs, so they are not a good trading source.

While at Fertility, Eiu made an agreement with Moses to sell him the extra rabbit fur. The bootmaker wants the fur. This will provide an additional income stream for the homestead. If Eiu can determine what is causing so many losses, he will have more rabbits to sell. Eiu has created data charts about each doe and her litter. He catalogs the age of each doe, the buck she mates with, the number of kittens, and how many live. They also record the types of illnesses and deaths that occur. Knowing how many kittens an individual doe can feed has led Eiu to remove some kittens and place them with another doe or bottle-feed them. He has checked out Lewis' public library books on the subject and talked to local veterinarians. Eiu found that moving his rabbits into hutches reduces the number of kids dying within the first four to six weeks. This takes a lot more room and cleaning time. Since this is Eiu's side project, he must use his resources and time wisely. Ateq has taken on some of his chores, but his available time is also limited. Eiu also culls the rabbits at a younger age to reduce the population. Adiu also set up hutches for her rabbits.

The community members on the western road don't hunt, so they are pleased when Adiu gives them rabbits. Eiu travels to the community with Doc Masterson to deliver the rabbits, starter hutches, and feed when he comes for birthing season and harvest. More families join the Western Road community as the Universal

Alliance government takes over their land to the east. More experienced families teach the men how to till the land. The lobby of the mail delivery office fills with double steel plows shortly after a new group arrives. Ateq and Eiu can't spend as much time as they would like at Adiu's homestead. Their mamatus and papatus are getting older, making them take longer to visit family members. Sometimes, only Ateq can come.

***

In 2166, a blight strikes the grain fields of Fertility and its neighbors. The homesteads under the mountain range are also affected. All the stalks must be pulled up and burned, the ground covered in lime, and left fallow for several years. Adiu can ride out this situation because she is single. She helps the townspeople with her surplus, and Eiu brings additional supplies during the harvest. Completing the harvest with just two people is difficult, but handling the crisis also leaves Adiu and Eiu drained.

One day, Adiu feels dizzy and nauseous. Talking with Eiu, they decide she is overworked and should slow down a little. The following day, Eiu throws up in the bathroom and passes out from the effort. Adiu finds him on the floor after the Morning Meal bell rings. She pulls him into a sitting position. Eiu is groggy but awake. They bridle the billy goats and pull themselves into the front seat. Adiu snaps the reins to get the goats going. Eiu leans over the front of the driving board to throw up on the ground. The only thing keeping Adiu upright in her seat is the buggy wall. Eventually, Eiu has nothing left in his stomach, so he leans back in the seat. Eiu feels the bumps in the road as the buggy moves. Looking over at Adiu, he sees her skin is bright red, her eyes are swollen shut, and her lips are cracked and bleeding. When Eiu touches Adiu, she doesn't respond. He tries to call her name, but his throat burns like it is on fire. Every bone feels like it is breaking. Eiu passes out again.

Later, Eiu feels someone brush against his body and hears distant voices. When he tries to open his eyes, there are only small slights of light. Eiu's breaths are labored and shallow. The voices continue around him as he feels himself being lifted. Eiu wants to sleep, but someone keeps shaking him. Eiu hears tires leaving the tar road and landing on gravel. Then nothing.

***

Eiu slowly awakens. He tries to move but can't. The brightness hurts his eyes when he attempts to open them. A loud grunt escapes Eiu's lips as he tries to free himself from whatever holds him in place. "We will have none of that," a male voice says. "I was wondering how long you would be out."

Somewhere in the back of his mind, the voice sounds familiar. Where have I heard that voice before?

194

"I imagine you are still pretty groggy. You and Adiu gave us quite a scare." A pair of glasses fall into place in front of his eyes and around his ears. "Try to open your eyes now."

Eiu opens his eyes slowly, expecting pain, but the glasses are heavily tinted. Dr. Masterson is looking down at him. "Oh, it is you. I wasn't able to place your voice."

"Lie back, Eiu; I will remove your restraints," Dr. Masterson says.

"What happened, and where am I? Where is Adiu, and how is she?" he asks.

"Nurse Kennedy, will you give me a hand with these? Eiu, don't move until I tell you to do so, and only how I tell you." When the restraint pressure against his body is removed, sharp bolts of pain take its place. Eiu attempts to keep his body still, but spasms run through his legs and arms to his fingers and toes.

"What you are experiencing are muscle spasms. This happens when someone fights the restraints for a long period, and the pressure is released. I am going to give you something to relax your muscles. That should help with the pain in your arms and legs. Don't worry; it is natural and has a low dose," says Dr. Masterson.

"What about Adiu?" Eiu asks again.

"I will tell you later. Right now, I need to know what you remember."

Eiu tries to think back, but there are only two images. "I am having trouble, Doc. In my head, I see Adiu and me talking at the homestead. She doesn't look good. Then I see us bridling the goats," Eiu says.

"Let me fill in the few details I know," Doc says. "Moses found the goats and wagon stopped in the middle of the road in front of the mail delivery office. You and Adiu were unconscious in the front seat. He went inside and told Jacob. Jacob called me and the paramedics. I decided we should wear infection-prevention suits before taking you out of the buggy. The paramedics placed your heads in neck braces and gently strapped each of you on a backboard. I checked your vital signs. You had high fevers with chills. Your bodies were swollen, and your lips were cracked. Adiu's lips were bleeding. I called ahead to Columbia Hospital. The infectious diseases specialist was waiting for us when we arrived. You were in isolation rooms for the first several days. Dr. Lehman ran tests, including taking spinal fluid. The test results indicated a severe viral infection. Fortunately, you were treated early enough, and neither lost any parts of your limbs."

"Slow down, Doc. You thought what we had might be contagious? How severe is this virus? You sound like that isn't the whole story, Eiu says.

Dr. Masterson says, "Wearing the preventive gear was just a precaution. I wasn't sure what caused your symptoms without examining you. Left untreated, this virus can require amputation of fingers, toes, hands, feet, arms, and legs. And in its most severe form, it can be deadly. But, as I said, we caught it early. When your temperature and blood pressure normalized, we assessed the damage the virus had done. Both of you required surgery. You needed it twice. You vomited so often with such violence your stomach acid came up your esophagus and into your mouth, burning the tissue. You also broke two ribs, locked your sternum in an upward position, and required thirty stitches on your forehead. Your first surgery relieved the pressure on your brain from the swelling."

"After tearing out your intravenous line, fracturing both forearms, breaking several fingers and toes, realigning your nose, and bruising most of your body during a seizure, Dr. Lehman decided to restrain you. A facial specialist did surgery on your nose. I splinted your fingers and toes before casting both forearm and hands. While you were under sedation, we ran additional tests. After speaking to a brain specialist, it was decided you have a chronic brain disorder as a result of the viral infection. This will be a permanent condition. You are on medication to reduce the risk of convulsions. Dr. Wagner, the brain specialist, will meet with you to explain the details, treatments, and changes to your diet that you may require," says Dr. Masterson. "The virus affected Adiu more severely than you. She was comatose when we took her from the buggy. She is still not awake."

"I contacted your father. The women are at Adiu's homestead, while the men tend to things at home. Although I didn't understand a single word she said, I took it from Equo's tone that she wasn't pleased when I told her no one was allowed to visit."

"You are fortunate you are not family. She may have taken a whip to you. Mama doesn't take being told she can't do something lightly," Eiu says, chuckling at the thought. "Please apologize to everyone on my behalf for all the trouble I caused."

"You are one strong person. It took six orderlies and two nurses to hold you while I sedated you. You fought the restraints in your sleep as well. Your body has been in a brawl for the last week. The staff understands that your brain is sending out the wrong signals. I would hate to be on your wrong side," says Doc.

"A week?" Eiu asks.

"Yes, you have been in the hospital for a week and will probably remain here for another. Get some rest. I want to start you on fluids and soft foods, then work you up to solids in a few days. I will check on you in the morning. The local chaplain will stop by. His degree is in morals and ethics. I think you will find him interesting. I am going to see Adiu later. I will let you know if anything changes," Dr. Masterson says as he leaves Eiu's room.

***

About forty-five minutes later, the nurse enters his room with a pitcher and a cup. She pours a small amount of tepid water into the cup. For the first time, Eiu realizes he has three splinted fingers and a cast on his right hand and forearm. He has the same cast without the splints on his left hand. The nurse holds the cup while Eiu drinks through a straw. An intravenous needle and line poke into the skin inside his right elbow. Eiu touches his swollen stomach with his left hand, simultaneously causing two things. He can feel his bladder and rectum release their waste. Eiu tries to stop the flow, but the forces are too strong. Fortunately, his catheter catches his urine. But brown fluid floods his sheets. Eiu feels even worse when the nurse calls an orderly to lift him while she removes his gown and washes Eiu clean with warm water from a bowl with soap. A second orderly brings a clean gown, sheets, and pillowcases. Redressed, the first orderly places him gently into a nearby chair while the nurse makes his bed.

"Sir, I think you should remain in bed until we get your diarrhea under control," the nurse says. "Don't be upset. It happens often after surgery."

The orderly agrees, "Happened to me when I had knee surgery. It took two orderlies to lift me. Being the well-fed man I am," he says as he rubs his stomach.

Later, Eiu is sitting up in his bed with his eyes closed. Suddenly, he feels like the bed is spinning. Then, his whole body stiffens like a board. He concentrates on hitting the red call button while his entire body spasms. The orderlies hold him firmly until the spasms end. Eiu is exhausted. Dr. Wagner, the brain specialist, enters his room about thirty minutes later. He gives Eiu medication in his intravenous line. They discuss how he acquired this disease, treatments, and changes to his diet that will reduce the number and severity of these episodes. Eiu will also be moved to a new room on the same floor as Dr. Wagner's office. The specialized staff will be observing him for the next thirty-nine hours. They will run additional tests.

***

Once relocated, Dr. Wagner's Physician's Assistant enters Eiu's room with a bowl of water, soap, a razor, and a cap with large round discs attached. She explains she will need to shave his head so the electrodes on the cap will pick up the signals Eiu's brain sends. He will be wearing the cap while under observation. With the cap in place, the physician's assistant injects medication into his intravenous line. Shortly, Eiu falls into a deep sleep.

When he wakes up, Eiu realizes he is back in restraints. He can't feel the cap against his head. A nurse arrives just a moment later. She says, "I will remove the head restraint now. Dr. Wagner would like the other restraints to remain in place for another few days. He will be in later to discuss the observation and test results. Would you like to sit up?"

"I think I will just stay lying down for now," Eiu replies.

"The chaplain has been asking about you. I will let him know he can visit. Your father has been updated, but visitations are still restricted. I will be back shortly with your medication," the nurse says.

Eiu relaxes his body into the bed. His mind is without thoughts, feelings, or emotions. Something is telling him to be calm. Chaplin Titus enters his room as Eiu's nurse injects medication into his tube.

"Hello, Chaplin Twiligar. Don't get him excited or stay too long; we are still working out his treatment and medication," the nurse says.

"I will try, but I can't make any promises, he responds smiling. "Hello, Eiu. You are a tough person to visit. As Nurse Opal said, I am Chaplin Twiligar. Please call me Titus. I try to assist patients during their time at the hospital with moral and ethical questions; failing that, I try to make their stays a little more comfortable. Can you give me an idea of your moral or ethical beliefs?"

"Titus, that is easy. Before meeting my partner-to-be, Adiu, I did my best to treat others as I wanted to be treated. After meeting with her to work on our partnership contract, I began studying *The No Fir* and learning the ancestral tongue. Doc Masterson said you studied these as well."

In response, Titus says, "I have. It is interesting how many communities have similar basic beliefs. I find the Ancestors' Children are the least dogmatic and accepting members of society. They probably also have the most right not to be. Almost all other communities are patriarchal. This leads to the more stereotypically masculine view of people based on their ability to be successful and dismisses those who fail to meet their expectations. The Ancestors' Children community's leaders have the more stereotypically feminine view, seeing the potential in all people to do their best and love everyone. They also understand that a community is stronger when it is unified. I want to hear your story as someone who came from the City and entered this orthodox agrarian community."

"Why do you call the community The Ancestors' Children? I didn't know they had a specific name. I have never heard them call themselves anything," Eiu inquires.

"It is unlawful to be a religious or spiritual organization member, but you can choose how to live your life. Within these outside community circles, others call them the Ancestors' Children because they believe they are the children of the thirteen original couples created by the Fir On and speak their ancestral tongue. They also believe Fir On will know them by their actions, so no name is required. I am called a chaplain because chaplains discuss and counsel others about subjects outside of religious or spiritual matters. You may have met people who live differently, but you probably will not hear them say they are members of a religious or spiritual group," says Titus. The discussion of Eiu's experience continues at a volume only the two can hear, and it stops when others come into the room. Titus visits him for the next seven days. Eiu looks forward to this time with Titus, hoping their discussions can continue once he leaves the hospital. On his eleventh day on Dr. Wagner's floor, the tests are repeated for three days.

Chapter 21

Adiu's & Eiu's Outcomes
First Day, First Month 2167

The year Twenty-One Hundred Sixty-Seven begins without either Adiu or Eiu to welcome its arrival. Adiu remains in a coma, and Eiu is sedated. To determine if medication, treatment, and dietary changes are positively affecting the quantity and severity of his seizures, Dr. Wagner's staff conducts a second round of testing. Adiu and Eiu have been in the hospital for twelve days. Their mama and mamatus care for Adiu's homestead, while Papa and the papatus work at Mama's and Papa's homestead. With so many unknowns, Mama and Papa make decisions concerning specific aspects of both homesteads. After weaning the last litter of kittens, they harvest the adult rabbits on both homesteads.

This reduction of daily chores results in the end of Eiu's additional income stream. Chicks remain after killing all the roosters and older hens. Additional refrigeration resources are acquired.

Mama visits Adiu and Eiu on the first day of the new year. She travels with Doctor Masterson, who comes to the hospital on his rounds every few days. Mama sits outside their rooms. In the outside world, openly praying is considered an act of defiance against the Universal Alliance government, so Mama places a book purchased from the hospital's gift store in front of her. Every so often, she turns a page to appear that she is reading. If someone turned her in, Mama could go to prison. The Universal Alliance government usually limits its reach to citizens in the cities and towns, but it is always better to be cautious.

While she is sitting outside Eiu's room waiting for Dr. Wagner and his staff to finish their tests, a nurse walks up to Mama.

She asks, "Mrs. Equo Udon Uoea?"

"Yes, may I help you?" Mama replies.

"I am Nurse Miriam. I am Doctor Masterson's Physician's Assistant. He asked me to find you. Please come with me."

When they arrive at Adiu's room, Dr. Masterson is already there. Adiu is sitting upright in a chair next to her bed. "You must take a special shower and wear a white suit like the staff, but you may see your daughter," Nurse Miriam says as she leads Equo to the sterilization room.

Dr. Masterson says, "Adiu, you scared me, and I don't scare easily. This is not the way I wanted your first visit to go. Moses found your buggy and goats standing in the middle of the street. He ran into the mail delivery office and asked Jakob to call me. When Moses described your condition, I had the paramedics meet me. We used infection prevention suits because I didn't know what had caused you to be this ill. Due to the awkward position of your body, they placed your head in a neck brace and your entire body on a backboard. You were running a very high temperature. Your body was swollen, and your lips were cracked to the point of bleeding. We transferred you by ambulance to the hospital here in Columbia. Dr. Lehman, a contagious disease specialist, and I ran a series of tests, including the removal of spinal fluid. We determined that you had a severe viral infection. If left unchecked, it can result in the amputation of whole or partial limbs, including toes, fingers, hands, feet, arms, or legs. In extreme cases, even death. Fortunately, we were able to treat it early. You required the complete or partial removal of several internal organs. Five internal medicine surgical teams completed the work. They removed your gall bladder, appendix, one of your kidneys, and parts of your reproductive system, intestines, bladder, and liver. Surgery also relieved the pressure on your brain from the swelling. As a result, you have neuromuscular damage as well. You will be required to wear leg braces and use forearm crutches. When we found you, you were non-responsive. You have been in a coma for more than twelve days. I will run tests to see if the medications have eradicated the virus and determine the severity of your neuromuscular damage. Until your immunity system returns to normal, you will remain in an intensive care unit floor isolation room. We will talk more later. You have a visitor."

Looking toward her door, Adiu sees someone in a white suit enter her room. She cannot see the person's face, but whoever she sees is straining to walk toward her—step, slide, step, slide, step, and slide. The person eventually stops just before Adiu's feet. She releases a giggle that causes her to wince in pain.

Seeing this, the person in the white suit says, "Daughter, do you know how long you have been in here? What did you do to make them think you are so frail?" in the ancestral tongue.

"Mama!" Adiu says as she reaches her arms out from under the covers of her bed.

"They said no visitors. I told the doctor, "I am your mama and will see you if I want." He acted like he didn't understand. I said, "You're a doctor. You understand me just fine. You think I don't know this. You had better do your best for my daughter, or I will beat you with my whip." Then Mamatu Ueon told me, "This is a place of business. Do you want those people to think all homesteaders are so badly tempered? Even if he doesn't understand your words, your tone came through. The doctor will let us know when we can see them. Such a fuss! I should have told you

Planet Thirteen – Adiu & Jotre

no more often when you were a child. You should be ashamed of yourself." We went back to your homestead and waited until the doctor told us I could go to the hospital with him. Enough about me. What trouble did you get yourself into now?" Mama says.

Adiu spends a long time explaining the events that occurred. Then she asks if Mama has seen Eiu.

Mama replies, "Just from outside his room. They are running special tests on Eiu. A strange man approached me while I was praying and tapped me on the shoulder. He speaks the ancestral tongue, but it isn't his first language. He says he is a chaplain at the hospital. He spoke so softly that I had to listen carefully to understand him. His name is Titus Twiligar. He offered to pray with me. I became so scared. What if this is a trick? I have been cautious. I bought a book from the gift shop and pretend to read it while secretly praying. You know the penalty for praying in public. I would be very unhappy in prison. They would not treat me nicely either."

"Mama, you are very smart about such things. I am sure you have taken every precaution possible. If someone had told the Universal Alliance government's undercover spies about you, you would not have been able to enter my room. I will ask Doc about the chaplain when he comes by later. I am getting tired. Do you mind if I close my eyes for a while, Mama?" says Adiu.

208

Mama says, "If you must. I will stay with you. You couldn't see my face until we were close, so I can pray without worrying if someone sees me."

Leaning back against her pillows, Adiu's eyes close, and she falls asleep immediately. Sometime later, nightmares invade her dreams, each concerning Eiu's departure from her life. Adiu thinks: Why now? Is my subconscious trying to tell me something? I care deeply about Eiu. He promised Qyn to pay me for what I spent on our broken partnership contract, an honorable trait in a partner. After Eiu paid his debt, we were able to be partners. He insisted on waiting. I honored Eiu's promise to do this with my own promise. We have less than seven years. Why are thoughts of losing Eiu haunting me so? If she knew, Mama would tell me I am causing myself stress for no reason. I am not in control; only the Fir On is. My responsibility is to pray. Mama is right. The staff has enough to do without me making such a fuss. Why is it that when things do not go the way I plan, I pass out or have nightmares that get to the point that I am screaming so loudly that Doc prescribed a sleep aid? Mama taught me to do better. Is my faith in the Fir On really this fragile?

When he visits, Adiu talks to Titus about the nightmares and their meaning. They speak in the ancestral tongue.

Titus says, "You and Eiu have had a life-threatening illness from which you are still recovering. You were in a coma for an extended time, gone through a massive surgery with the removal or partial removal of seven internal body parts. That doesn't take into account the emotional and mental stress of dealing with the measures taken to save your life and the life of Eiu, someone you care deeply about. Adiu, I don't know if I would be only having nightmares. They did surgery to relieve pressure on your brain from the swelling. I think you need to give yourself a break. I have been in this hospital long enough to know the staff has dealt with a lot worse than a patient screaming. Would you allow me to pray for you out loud?"

"Will you pray for Eiu also?" Adiu asks.

Titus grips the railing on Adiu's bed while she locks her fingers together in her lap. "Fir On, we are grateful for your blessings in these difficult times. I ask for your assistance in convincing Adiu that she is enough, has done enough, and to stop trying to handle everything. You do it better and don't need someone interfering. This also goes for Eiu, who thinks he knows better than his doctors regarding being discharged. Please give them boring lives for a while."

Adiu cannot stop smiling at his words: "I hear you and Mama have become secret prayer partners. Her accent takes over when she is excited and thicker when she is fighting against the Universal Alliance government. There is a reason Papa keeps her away from the outside world. Mama feels so happy to have a conspirator who knows her language and is willing to take risks."

"I know where I would place my bet in that fight. Has Equo Udon Uoea always been so contentious?" Titus asks.

Adiu replies, "Mama has mellowed with age. Papa's mama, Mamatu Udon does not like that he paid a substantial amount of money to Mama's matchmaker to move Papa to the top of the list. She had other plans at the time. She still blames Mama. Mamatu Udon and Mama are alike in personality, temperament, and moral fortitude. No one risks telling them this. Papa knows he married a woman just like his papa did. He figures it works for Papatu Otau, so it works for him. Papa is an identical copy of his papa. I think that is why both couples have been married for so long. My mamatus and papatus live in a house on my parents' homestead. The two families owned adjacent homesteads for generations."

"Chaplain, you have been here long enough for today. Dr. Masterson wants Adiu to take her first walk to the shower using her braces and crutches. When our patients arrive, you barely share anything in common. Yet, by the end of their stay, you seem like old friends. You do have a gift. Now, off with you," the nurse says in City Speak, smiling at Titus.

Adiu slides into a pink sleep set from home after her shower. Mama brought it from Adiu's homestead. She also sent along her hair brush and comb.

***

After the Morning Meal, Adiu is moved off the intensive care unit and out of isolation. Her new staff wear standard uniforms without the infection prevention suits. A physical therapist wheels her to an exercise suite. Nanette teaches Adiu the proper technique for completing the exercises she will do three times daily at home. Cyrus, a magnetic resonance imaging technician, catches Adiu as she returns to her room. Spinning her around, they head to do a full body screening. Another nurse, Ira, arrives to take blood samples when Cyrus finishes.

Back in her room, Adiu gives urine and fecal samples. A postoperative care nurse checks her surgical scars and records her vitals in her chart. With everything that has occurred, Adiu's charts are the size of an encyclopedia volume for the letter S. Just before the Evening Meal, Dr. Masterson arrives.

Reading through the latest notes, Doc shakes his head. He says, "You have been poked, prodded, and paraded through the hallways enough for one day. I am waiting on today's test results. We will see what they have to say and how you are doing in therapy. I may order more tests depending on the results. I am keeping the intravenous line in. It makes it easier to give you higher doses of medication. I have ordered a specific post-operative diet for you. Please eat and drink as much of it as possible. You may feel nauseous or vomit. I added a prescription to combat this. I also added other medications to assist your digestion. Your vital signs show you should be through the worst and are on the mend.

But just in case, behave yourself. No relapsing. Doctor's order." It is the first time Adiu has seen Doc smile since she woke up in the hospital.

"How is Eiu?" Adiu asks.

"Dr. Wagner continues to monitor his progress."

Adiu says, "Please tell me more. I need to know."

"I cannot do that. By law, I am required not to share another patient's information with anyone but their immediate family. I have contacted his father, who is his only legal family member. Just as I do for you and my other patients, I recommended he keep that information between his wife and himself. They make decisions about his care based on the information I give them. The town of Columbia, and by extension, the Universal Alliance government, controls this hospital. I have medical privileges here at their discretion. It is a fine line to walk. I won't risk losing this hospital's resources," Dr. Masterson says. At this moment, Adiu understands Mama's concerns better.

Adiu adjusts her behavior accordingly until Doc's car arrives in Fertility upon her release from the hospital five days later.

Chapter 22

Adiu's Homecoming
Eighth Day, First Month, 2167

Looking through the windows of Dr. Masterson's automobile, Adiu wonders where the people of Fertility are. Then she remembers: This is the Sabbath. Everyone is either in church or at home. Even the restaurant is closed. It will be nice to go home and quietly relax.

Adiu had been so concerned about her behavior under Columbia's dome that she forgot to inquire about Eiu.

"Doc, where is Eiu?" Adiu asks.

Doc says, "Eiu is at your homestead. He was released a few days ago. Do you understand why I was unable to tell you before? ***Recently, there have been changes in the Universal Alliance government. Columbia's local government publicly says it is independent, but some high-ranking townspeople have their primary homes and businesses in the larger cities. Most of these people have risen through the city's social ranks within the last ten to twenty years. Cities and towns annex land farther and farther from their centers instead of creating new towns."

Doc and Adiu enter the access road to Adiu's homestead. Just like everyone else, he is amazed by its entranceway. The womenfolk are waiting as Doc and Adiu reach the house. They act like they never doubted Adiu would return, leaving her to walk alone—instead, the swarm attacks Doc. One opens the driver's side door before the engine stops completely. They lead Doc inside, making a fuss over who is nearest to him. In unison, they tell Eiu to make way, gesturing with their hands and arms.

"I apologize for not finding a way to see you, but everyone thinks it was for the best," Eiu says.

Adiu replies, "Doc explained the risks. I am glad to see you now. I hope Doc can handle this much admiration."

"In their minds, he is THE excellent healing instrument sent by Fir On to save their children from the consequences of their silly actions. With you back home, they can focus their disappointment and chastisement on you for a while," Eiu says.

Adiu says, "You are not even close to being out of trouble. Between them, they have more than enough skills to make us feel bad for a long time."

Adiu and Eiu's conversation continues for the next hour as

they sit on benches at an outside table. They share their experiences in the hospital, the changes they need to make, and future medical events.

The mighty hero, Dr. Masterson, escapes the house, but only with an entourage of women carrying bags and boxes of food in his wake. They load their parcels into the passenger's side front seat, the entire backseat, and most of the automobile's trunk. Then, based on their rank in the family, they hug him and place a kiss on his forehead. Even after he leaves Adiu's entranceway and can't be seen, the women still talk about him.

***

Mama gives Adiu and Eiu a wary eye but returns with the others to the house. After she is gone, they are silent for a moment.

Adiu says, "While I was in the hospital, I started having nightmares."

"I am so sorry. What are they about? Do you know what is causing them?" Eiu asks.

Adiu says, "My nightmares are about you. Most specifically about losing you. You are fulfilling your promise to Qyn. I appreciate that you take your promises seriously. You have six and a half more years. I promised to wait for you, but I think my desire not to wait is the cause of my nightmares."

Eiu looks startled. "You have changed your mind. I understand. I am not the same man you made that promise to. I told you then, and I am telling you now, whether you wait or not, I will keep my promise," he says.

Adiu says, "I am a different woman than I was then. You paid the debt required by *The No Fir* and the expenses you and your mother incurred. I chose to spend the money for the remainder. Those were my expenses to pay whether we became partners or not."

"I promised to repay you. That is still my choice," Eiu replies.

Adiu says with tears running down her cheeks, "Please. I am pleading with you. Do not go back. Stay here with me. I do not care about the money. I never have. Be my partner now."

Eiu brushes the tears away with the back of his fingers. "I need to talk to Mama."

He gets up from the table and runs to the front door. In a moment, their mamatus walk to the bench, sitting on either side of Adiu. They take turns holding her in their arms, whispering in her ear. Eventually, Adiu falls asleep, worn out from crying. The mamatus see Eiu leave the house, walking toward the yurt. After a short explanation, Mama hitches the goats to the buggy. The mamatus carry Adiu into the first bed chamber and onto the bed.

***

Adiu awakens to the smell of food cooking and the sound of female voices. The women are canning fruit and vegetables in glass jars in the kitchen. She sits down at the dining area table to watch. Mama brings her a bowl of vegetable soup and a glass of goat's milk.

"The vegetables are from your garden," says Mama.

Mama waits patiently as Adiu prays and eats. After eating genetically modified meals for so long, she relishes each bite.

Mama says, "Eiu has taken a train back to our homestead. He is not permitted to stay. We talked about your request. Eiu has a tough decision to make, with many different consequences. The Matron and our community must be consulted. Contact will come when the situation has been handled. For now, we have things to do."

Adiu wants to ask more questions, but she knows Mama has said all she will say about the subject. Adiu grabs her stomach, feeling ill. Turning away from the table, her vomit pours into the empty bowl in her hands. Mama hands her a dish towel. Adiu wipes her face and hands. Her mamatus help her into the first bed chamber and night clothes. Once Adiu is under the covers, Mama enters carrying a syringe. She sticks its needle into her arm and pushes the plunger.

Questions begin forming in Adiu's mind. Where did Mama learn to do that? What was in the syringe? I have so many questions.

Then nothing.

***

Ateq picks up Eiu at the shuttle stop. He remains quiet on the ride, seeing Eiu is deep in thought. Qyn's response to Mama's telegram lies on the dining area table. She will see Eiu and Papa tomorrow after the Midday Meal. Papa calls from one of the barns for assistance. Ateq and Eiu head there. The remainder of the day is spent on daily chores. Eiu helps where he can.

Papa asks Ateq and Eiu to stay at the dining area table after the meal.

Ateq translates the conversation. "We are happy to see you looking so good. Mama doesn't like to spend money unnecessarily, so we didn't receive much information. I have contacted the community about Adiu's request. They are consulting *The No Fir* and praying for guidance. I would not expect any responses until tomorrow. This is a complicated matter. Is this the way things usually are for you?" Papa asks.

Eiu replies, "It appears that Adiu has this effect on my life." They all smile. During Wisdom studies, they all pray for guidance.

Many responses come the following day. Some of them are questions, while others are recommendations. Papa reads these while waiting at the Matron Family Services' office.

<u>Lancaster Telegram & Telephone Co.</u>

To: Iuot Udon Otau
From: Ante Eoud Otau Udon & Family

Is there a difference in commitment if the promise is verbal or written?

<u>Lancaster Telegram & Telephone Co.</u>

To: Iuot Udon Otau
From: Ante Aoud Otau Udon & Family

Does it matter if Eiu made the promise to the Matron and not to Adiu directly?

<u>Lancaster Telegram & Telephone Co.</u>

To: Iuot Udon Otau
From: Mamatre Eaoc & Family

Adiu has dishonored Eiu by asking him to break his promise. Eiu needs to consider carefully whether the Fir On wants him to partner with a woman of such character.

<u>Lancaster Telegram & Telephone Co.</u>

To: Inot Udon Otau
From: Mamatu Otau & Family

Paying the dowry amount was a legal agreement between Adiu and Eiu. The additional payment is a moral obligation. Legally, Eiu has met his obligation, so this is not a reason for delaying the partnership. The issue surrounds his morals. Eiu made this promise knowing the cost. He needs to fulfill his responsibility. Does this impact when the partnership occurs? We are of two different minds. Our final thought is that Adiu and Eiu need to wait.

<u>Lancaster Telegram & Telephone Co.</u>

To: Inot Udon Otau
From: Oeat Etiq Atua & Family

Although the promise was made in good faith at the time, circumstances have changed enough that it should be reevaluated.

Lancaster Telegram & Telephone Co.

To: Iuot Udon Otau
From: Ioeq Ouas Eqae & Family

*As partners, Eiu fulfills his monetary obligations because Adiu
will be the head of the household.*

Lancaster Telegram & Telephone Co.

To: Iuot Udon Otau
From: Mamatu Ueon & Family

*Since Eiu has paid the debt requested by Adiu and half of the
amount he promised, could an agreement be written for Eiu to meet
his remaining promised obligation after becoming partners?*

Lancaster Telegram & Telephone Co.

To: Iuot Udon Otau
From: Ante Aoud Otau Udon & Family

*Does it matter if Eiu made the promise to the Matron and not
to Adiu directly?*

<u>*Lancaster Telegram & Telephone Co.*</u>

To: Iuot Udon Otau
From: Mamatre Eatu & Family

The first issue in this relationship concerned Eiu's name. This time, the problem is Adiu's want. It will happen if Fir On's desires a partnership. If not, it was not meant to be. Adiu and Eiu should wait.

Papa sends Mama a telegram summarizing all the questions and answers. As Eiu's only legal family member, Papa must make a recommendation, and Mama, the head of the household and Adiu's mother, must do so also. If Mama and Papa disagree, this could cause conflict between them.

Mama calls Qyn's office from Moses' telephone in his office. Papa takes her call in the meeting room. He waits patiently for Mama to finish talking before he begins.

Mama says, "If the Matron agrees to a contract amendment for the remaining amount to be given after the partnership ceremony, Adiu and Eiu do not need to delay."

Mama also gives Papa a list of tasks that he must complete while he is in Ephrata. Mama continues, "Eiu must remain at their homestead until then. I will talk to Adiu after Eiu has made his decision."

Papa walks down to Qyn's office to deliver the news. Based

upon this turn of events, Qyn will take time to consider her decision. Papa and Eiu head back to the homestead. There is still work to be done before the Evening Meal.

***

Eiu receives another telegram from Qyn. This time, she wants to meet with Papa and Eiu in her office to discuss her decision.

What happens if Qyn says we can be partners sooner? Is that what I want? How will it reflect on me and my family if I choose to do this? Will this negatively affect Adiu in our community? I don't want anyone to think negatively about her. I understand why Adiu wants this. I was dealing with the separation, but now I don't want to wait to be with her. Who will take care of Adiu if I am not there? There are so many questions. These and more questions are plaguing Eiu as they enter her office.

"Iuot and Eiu, please have a seat," Qyn says in City Speak and the ancestral tongue. "I have consulted matrons within and outside my family. I also contacted several contract lawyers for their opinions. This unusual situation requires careful consideration as it will set a precedent. I can justify many opinions depending on a person's interpretation of *The No Fir*, the community's responses, and legality under the Universal Alliance Government's laws. Before giving a decision, I have some questions."

"Iuot, you and Equo have prayed to Fir On for guidance,

consulted others, referred to *The No Fir*, arriving at a shared conclusion based on your interpretation and beliefs. If I agree with you, are you willing to deal with any negative consequences for you as their parents, family, and community members?" Qyn asks.

Iuot replies, "We have considered this. We are."

"If I agree with your parents' proposed arrangement, Eiu, have you decided based on the possibility and its effects?" Qyn asks.

Eiu replies, "I am torn between my desire to be with Adiu as her partner now and fulfilling the promise I made to you. I told you once that I am the proud son of a moral man. You asked me if I am a son that a moral man would be proud of. That question and its answer have guided my choices every day since. I will accept any negativity towards myself, but I have a problem bringing it to my family and Adiu."

Qyn says, "I appreciate the seriousness your family and community have shown. I respect the amount of time and effort put forth. Here is my decision: Since you have fulfilled your monetary obligation for breaking the partnership contract with Adiu, you have met your legal responsibility. With the diverse responses from your community, you cannot satisfy all of their courses of action. Your family has made a recommendation and is willing to take any adverse consequences of following their advice. But this promise was made to me by you as a matron, so I think the burden falls upon us to resolve this dilemma. I also have prayed for and sought guidance from Fir On and *The No Fir*. As the receiving party of your promise, I have the right to request changes or revisions to your original promise. I will give you my response only if, on hearing it, you accept my conditions and the results of doing so without delay or question. Are you willing to do this?"

Thinking about her words, Eiu says, "Qyn, I need time to pray and consider your request. May I have privacy to do so?"

After translating Eiu's words for Iuot, Qyn and he stand up and leave the room. The door closes behind them. Eiu prays, "Fir On, you know my heart and those of everyone involved. Accepting Qyn's offer is a leap of faith. Not doing so could lead to many other outcomes. If you have an opinion, please share it with me. I will follow whatever you suggest."

Eiu remains still waiting. He receives his answer in time and searches for Qyn and Papa.

"Qyn, Fir On has spoken. I will do as you have asked. He has given his blessing on your decision," Eiu says.

Qyn replies, "You will set aside one-half of all profits due to you as Adiu's partner for the next six years as a penalty for fulfilling your promise after entering into a partnership with her. This money will remain hers only and cannot be used to meet the needs of your union. Adiu will hold this money as a commitment from you to her after you have preceded her in death."

"I don't understand. What half of all profits?" Eiu asks.

Iuot answers, "In a contracted partnership, the woman divides the yearly profits in several ways. The firstborn child receives one-half. The second child receives one-fourth, and so on until all the children have received their portion. Ateq receives one-fourth of the homestead's yearly profit as our second child, and you receive one-eighth as our third child. Once these are given, the remainder is divided equally between the partners. Each partner decides how to use their portion. Mama and I give twenty percent of our portions to the community to meet the needs of its members. We contribute twenty percent to a savings account and emergency fund each. We keep another fund for the surviving partner when one of us passes on. Mama sets aside another twenty percent for personal savings, with the remainder for her personal use. I also set aside twenty percent for my savings and the remainder for personal use. The Matron says you will give Adiu half of your portion of the annual profits for six years. This money will go into Adiu's surviving partner's fund. The remainder is available for you to use as you see fit. After six years, you have met your obligation to the Matron and your promise to Adiu. This will be an addition to your partnership contract."

"I didn't know that Mama's role in the family is this complicated. I gave you my word to do as you ask, so it will be," Eiu replies.

Qyn says, "This is called an amendment. Adiu needs to agree to the partnership contract with this change. I am placing a time constraint on the completion of the partnership for three calendar months. During this time, you will work with Equo to create a financial plan and to understand the roles Adiu and you will perform in your union. My staff will draft a new partnership contract. I will contact Adiu with the details and your decision. It will be her choice to accept these changes or to request any amendments of her own. Until the partnership ceremony, you will remain living apart."

Everyone shakes hands and hugs. Papa and Eiu take their leave.

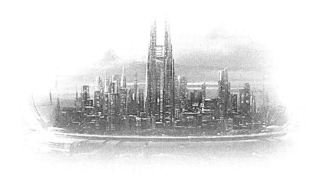

Chapter 23

Adiu's & Eiu's Partnership Ceremony
Thirteenth Day, Fourth Month, 2167

The following day, Adiu receives Qyn's telegram at the mail delivery service building. She gives the telegram to Mama. Mama reads it out loud in the ancestral tongue to her mamatus. As Adiu watches their faces for responses, all work stops. Mama leads Adiu and her mamatus to the dining area table. She bows her head, and her lips move in silent prayer. Looking around the table, Adiu sees her mamatus are also praying. She bows her head and begins silently: Fir On, my family, Qyn and our community have found a way for Eiu and I to be partners in three months. I thank you for your blessing upon Qyn's decision. I ask for your guidance during this time, so that I may prepare for joining this partnership with Eiu. I know this is not what Eiu had planned.

Please assist me with making this partnership one in which he will not regret entering early or at all. Bless Eiu with your love and understanding as he learns our roles in this partnership."

Returning to the mail delivery office building to send a telegram to Qyn, Adiu receives another telegram. Ateq requests he stay with Adiu at her homestead when Mama and their mamatus return home. Papa and their papatus miss their partners, and their absence will ruin the homestead if it lasts much longer. Ateq will assist Adiu with the daily chores until the partnership union ceremony.

Adiu calls Qyn's office from Jakob's telephone. A staff member answers. He will inform Qyn of Adiu's decision, and the amended partnership contract will be mailed the next day in the midday post. Adiu presents Ateq's telegram to Mama and her mamatus upon her return. While discussing Ateq's request, Adiu makes a checklist of things she must complete before the ceremony.

With her list started, Adiu hears the Midday Meal bell ring. She is still working out which foods she can eat without being ill and how much. Mama visited Doctor Masterson's office yesterday for a refill of her medications and a diet guide. She found out who the little girl is that Adiu met on her first visit to Doc's office. Her name is Magnolia. Her mama, Violet, is the doctor's on-call nurse. Violet, her husband, and their children live downstairs, so she can assist Doc whenever he needs her. Her husband, River, is Fertility's pharmacist. He has an office downtown near the restaurant.

Ateq arrives a few days later at Adiu's homestead. He is tired from the long trip alone. By sleeping in the wagon for a few hours each night by the side of the road, Ateq shortened his trip's time by several hours. He drops his things in the yurt. Mama heats water on the stove, and their mamatus carry a bucket of cold water from the stream, a natural sponge, and homemade soap. Mama made the tea leaf oil soap while Adiu and Eiu were hospitalized. Each bar is wrapped in waxed paper and tied with a thin rope ending in a bow. The mamatus crocheted scouring pads from tulle material as well. They all took turns making Adiu new clothing on her treadle sewing machine.

Before leaving the next day, Mama writes a list of chores Ateq needs to do. She also makes another one for Adiu. Mama had ordered and received a new spinning wheel and wool carding brush for Adiu. Mama lists sheep shearing and rabbit skinning for Ateq, wool carding, spinning, and clothing weaving for Adiu. Ateq is to take the rabbit furs to Moses for the bootmaker. Eiu will send additional furs to Moses from their parents' homestead.

With Adiu in forearm and leg braces, she moves carefully and slowly around the homestead. Adiu also tires quickly. She needs to take several breaks and split her work into smaller parts. Ateq had always worked with the family on their parents' homestead. The work required to maintain Adiu's homestead is almost overwhelming. Adiu and Ateq drop into their beds each night, exhausted, and fall asleep immediately.

Adiu receives and sends letters to Eiu during their three month separation. She and Ateq talk about the work he will complete while she is gone. Adiu has hired several townspeople's children to assist him.

***

Finally, the time comes for Adiu to leave her homestead and travel back to their parents. Adiu packs her bags the night before. Doc Masterson is giving her a lift to the train station in Paradise. The shuttle ride seems to Adiu to be taking forever. She has a four-hour wait before her train arrives at the station.

Adiu spends part of this time at the restaurant inside the station. She can eat more types of foods and larger quantities but is careful to order cream soup, a chicken salad sandwich on soft bread, iced tea, and water. For dessert, Adiu has vanilla pudding.

Adiu visits the small shops outside the train station, looking for a gift to give Qyn. She finds a black and red lacquered box with raised decorations cut into its lid. Inside, deep red silk covers the sides and bottom. The saleswoman wraps her purchase in cherry blossom tree paper and folds the paper into an origami design. Then she places it in a black silk bag with gold and green tree decorations. Adiu places Qyn's present in her satchel, making sure it will be safe during her trip by placing her soft night robe around it.

***

Mama waits for Adiu's train to arrive. She thinks Adiu is finally becoming a partner. For a long time, her papa and I didn't know this time would come for her. She has always been so strong and independent. We were not sure any man would be willing or able to be her partner. Eiu is a good choice for her.

Mama races down the station walkway when she sees Adiu exit the train. She grabs her bags from the train conductor and insists on carrying them for her. Adiu must rest on a bench for a few minutes as they walk to the entrance. Speaking in their ancestral tongue, Mama takes this opportunity to tell her every detail about the events at their homestead since she returned. Mama is still talking when they arrive at the homestead.

"Until after the ceremony, you will be staying with your mamatus and papatus. You can wait a few more days to be with Eiu. He has been told the same thing. I have made yours and Eiu's robes and stoles. He helped me with cutting out the pieces and pinning them together," Mama tells Adiu.

Her mamatus and papatus come out of the first barn. Adiu is passed around for hugs and needs to sit on the edge of the wagon bed to catch her breath. The mamatus take Adiu's arms and lead her to their house. The papatus carry her bags. The entire walk, they ask Adiu questions. She can barely give one answer before another question comes her way. Mamatu Ueon pulls a chair at the dining area table and seats Adiu. Mamatu Udon places a plate of soft foods and a glass of water before her. Papatu Uoea and Papatu Otau return from the sitting room. The questioning continues right where it left off on their walk to the house after Adiu prays.

They only end after Adiu says, "The journey was long, and I am quite tired. Can we continue this discussion after I have had a good night's sleep?"

Guiltily, her mamatus lead Adiu into the sitting area where a cot has been set up for her to sleep in. Adiu realizes the design on the top quilt has cross-stitched hearts with Eiu's and her names and the date of their partnership ceremony. Adiu begins to cry and hugs each of her mamatus and papatus tightly. She is just finished preparing for bed and leaving the bathroom when Adiu turns around from shutting off the light and bumps into someone in front of her. Adiu looks up into a pair of gold rings around black circles. She stands frozen in her place. Eiu takes Adiu in his arms and holds her tight. A throat clears behind him.

"If Mama catches you here, Adiu will attend your funeral, not your partnership ceremony. She sent me to find you. Mama wants you to try on your robe and stole one more time," Ateq says.

Eiu releases Adiu from his hold but leans over to kiss her forehead. Red spreads across both their faces.

Ateq says, "Enough of that. Mama will kill all of us if she finds out. Time to go."

"Good night, Eiu."

"Good night, Adiu, and sweet dreams." Ateq shoves Eiu through the front door and out into the yard.

Mamatu Ueon smiles at Papatu Uoea as he rolls his eyes upward. Papatu Otau kisses Mamatu Udon before she smacks him, and they return from their hiding places behind their bed chamber doors.

***

The day of their partnership ceremony arrives. Ateq will remain behind at the homestead to prepare for the partnership celebration. Qyn sends two carriages to pick up the rest of the family. The men leave the homestead first. Eiu is dressed in his dark red robe and matching stole. The ladies are following, with Adiu in her dark blue robe and stole.

As soon as the carriages leave the homestead, wagons filled with members of the orthodox homesteader community enter.

Ateq tries to assist, but he gets in the way more than anything else. Eventually, Ateq heads to the barns to check on the animals.

***

At the Matron Family Services' office, the largest staff room is illuminated by candles surrounding its interior. Qyn stands at the far end of the room, awaiting the participants.

Adiu and Equo enter first, followed by Mamatu Ueon and Mamatu Udon. Equo stands to the right of Adiu on the right side of Qyn, while the mamatus are seated on chairs on the right side of the aisle. Iuot and Eiu enter, with Papatu Otau and Papatu Uoea just behind them. Iuot stands to the left of Eiu on the left side of Qyn, and the papatus are seated on the left side of the aisle.

Forty-five minutes later, Qyn opens the staff room doors and leads the partnered couple into her office to sign their partnership license. Mama and Papa serve as legal witnesses with their signatures. Qyn's staff has prepared a small celebration in another staff room. A tower of petit fours sits on a table, and Byn's fermented fruit "hooch" is poured into crystal glasses with ice.

Qyn says in City Speak, "Congratulations to Mrs. Adiu Equo Iuot and Mr. Eiu Iuot Otau. May Fir On bless your lives together from this day forward." She repeats this in the ancestral tongue.

Glass clinks against one another. The party members take a drink and place petit fours in their mouths.

Adiu presents Qyn with the gift she purchased at the train station. Showing the others her gift, Qyn tears up and beams with joy. The women gather around her to see Adiu's gift and comment on its outstanding qualities. Adiu is pleased that Qyn and the others like her gift. Eiu is talking to one of the staff members when Adiu comes up behind him and taps Eiu's shoulder. When he turns around, Adiu takes both sides of Eiu's face in her hands and kisses him deeply. Eiu kisses her back. A series of throat clearings and laughter serenade Adiu and Eiu. When the kiss ends, blushes appear on their cheeks. Mama turns to Papa and plants a kiss on his lips. Mamatu Ueon follows suit with Papatu Uoea, who looks very uncomfortable with her display of affection. Papatu Otau doesn't wait his turn; he swings Mamatu Udon around in a circle and leans her backward, kissing her nose. She pulls herself upright and smacks him on the shoulder. Everyone but Papatu Uoea and Mamatu Udon laugh. The party continues for half an hour. After making their farewells, the family loads back into the carriages. This time, Adiu, Eiu, Mama, and Papa ride together. The mamatus and papatus ride in the other carriage.

***

Arriving back at Equo and Iuot's homestead, the family members are met with cheering and hugs. The community members have brought their best dishes to the tables. After the meal and toasts for the new couple, Adiu and Eiu make the rounds to thank everyone for their generosity.

An hour into the festivities, several community members unpack their musical instruments. The music begins. Eiu is unprepared for this turn of events and looks sheepishly at Adiu. Adiu approaches him, places his hands in the proper positions, and leads Eiu around the dance floor. Adiu and Eiu glide around the yard, turning in circles as they proceed. Most of the partnered couples join them. Then bold single women find single men, and little girls grab little boys, dragging them into the circle. After two dances, Adiu and Eiu sit down to take a break.

***

Once they have recovered, Adiu leads Eiu by the hand to the front of their parents' house. Waiting, there is a wagon with a bridled horse. The bed is filled with their bags, presents, and equipment for their homestead. Adiu climbs into the driver's seat and picks up the reins. After a moment, Eiu joins her. Snapping the reins, Adiu leads the horse from their parents' homestead onto the north road. In a while, the wagon turns to the left and crosses the train line. Coming up in the town of Blue Ball, Adiu steers the wagon to an inn on the outskirts of the town.

Adiu jumps down from the driver's seat and collects her bags. Eiu does the same. He follows Adiu to the front desk. They take turns signing into the register. A desk clerk shows them to their room for the next seven nights.

End of Part Two & Book One

Characters

*** All vowels in the homesteaders' ancestral names are pronounced with a long vowel sound. ***

Adiu Equo Iuot (Ancestral Name) – Homesteader Firstborn daughter looking for a union partner.

Ateq Iuot Equo (Ancestral Name) – Adiu's younger homesteader brother.

Deba Mara Jotu/Aata Atau Ueqi (City Name/Ancestral Name) – Jotre's older deceased sister.

Equo Ueon Uoea (Ancestral Name) – Adiu & Ateq's mama & partner to Papa Iuot Udon Otau.

Isac Jotu Mara/Eqat Ueqi Atau (City Name/Ancestral Name) – Jotre's younger brother.

Iuot Uoea Otau (Ancestral Name) – Adiu & Ateq's papa & partner to Mama Equo Ueon Uoea.

Jotre Jotu Mara/Aeat Ueqi Atau/Eiu Iuot Otau (City Name/Original Ancestral Name/Adopted Ancestral Name) – Adiu's proposed union partner.

Jotu Joun Ruth/Ueqi Ueqa Udon (City Name/Ancestral Name) – Jotre's deceased father & partner to Mara Ana Hener.

Mamatre Eaoc (Ancestral Name) – Papatu Uoea's mama & partner to Papatre Osea.

Characters (Continued)

*** All vowels in the homesteaders' ancestral names are pronounced with a long vowel sound. ***

Mamatre Eatu (Ancestral Name) – Mamatu Otau's mama & widow.

Mamatu Otau (Ancestral Name) – Papa Iuot's mama & partner to Papatu Udon.

Mamatu Ueon (Ancestral Name) – Mama Equo's mama & partner to Uoea Osea Eaoc.

Mara Ana Hener/Atau Ionu Aeqi (City Name/Ancestral Name) – Jotre's mother.

Papatre Osea (Ancestral Name) – Papatu Uoea's papa & partner to Mamatre Eaoc.

Papatu Udon (Ancestral Name) – Papa Iuot's papa & partner to Mamatu Otau.

Papatu Uoea (Ancestral Name) – Mama Equo's papa & partner to Mamatu Ueon.

Acknowledgements

Melissa LaPlace supported me through one of the more difficult times of my working life with grace and great empathy. You are also the person who read my written work, was (good) surprised and gave me the confidence to pursue writing as a career.

Michelle Smith gave me the greatest advice, as a teacher and a person. She also taught me to loosen up, no one was going to die if I made a mistake.

Jeff Sutter guarded my heart and soul during difficult times and made me laugh at the weirdest things. He gave me spiritual guidance I still follow.

Kieren Westwood gave the best writing advice and convinced me I am a writer. As the editor of three chapters in this book, I found his suggestions thought-provoking and his questions provided clarity. He gives of himself readily to support other writers.

Alton Wirick gave me the time to find myself and my voice even when it was not financially wise to do so. Even if you don't understand, your love and support gives me the courage to learn more, do more, and be the best I can be.

Jacobie Wirick

Jacobie Wirick was born in Lancaster County, Pennsylvania and currently resides in Elkhart County, Indiana with her husband, Alton, and three rescued Chihuahua mix dogs. She has retired after fifty years, and is pursuing writing full-time.

Jacobie was first published as a college student at Indiana – Purdue at Fort Wayne (IPFW). Her final essay, "You May Be Philosophy Student If" was selected by her Critical Thinking class professor to be included in the next edition of his class textbook.

At the time of publication, Jacobie is working on the next novel in the Planet Thirteen series, *Wenona & Ateg*.

Jacobie.wirick@gmail.com

Made in the USA
Monee, IL
19 May 2025

17423898R00152